Guardians of Hydia

Facing the Past

Guardians of Hydia

Facing the Past

Alysha Stroud

First Printing: 2013

ISBN 978-0-9936566-0-6

This book is dedicated

to my parents,
Kevin and Shelley,

to my sister,
Belina,

and to my husband,
Andrew.

for their continued support and listening ear.

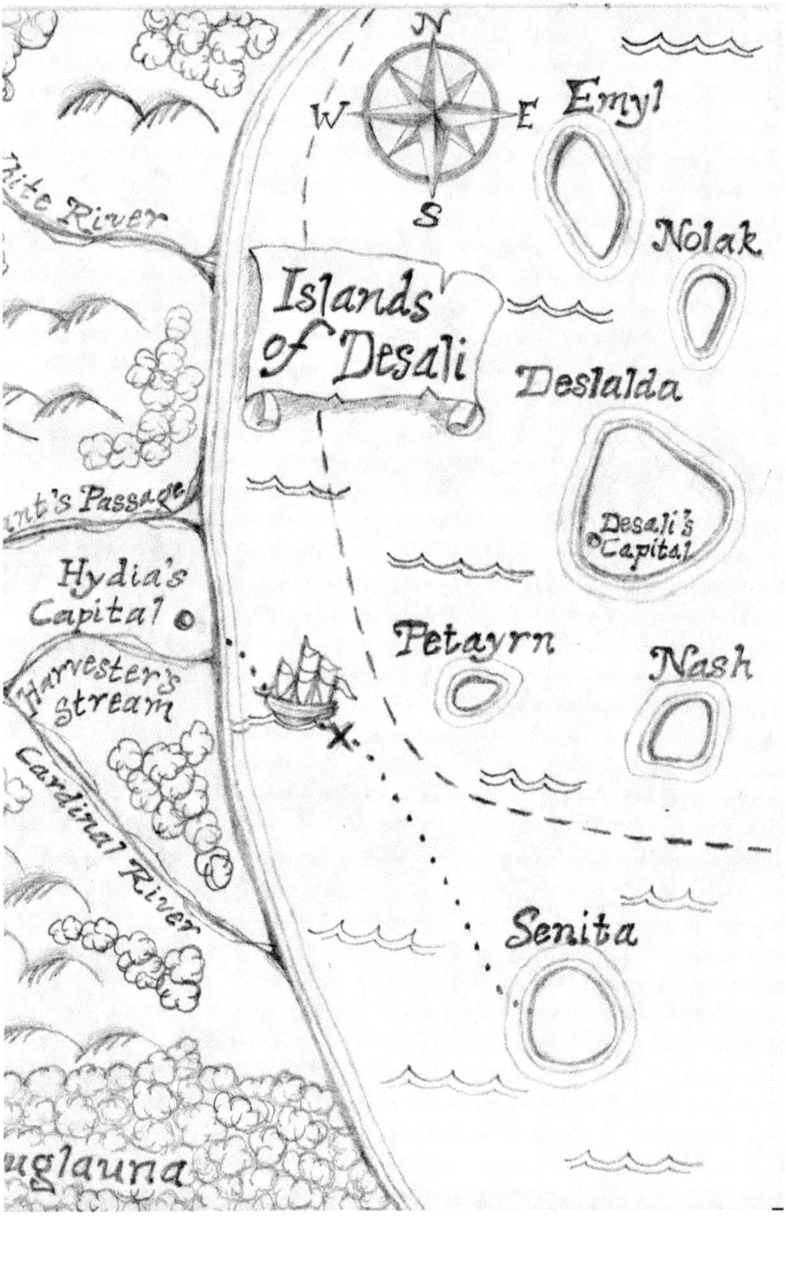
N
W
E
S
Emyl
Nolak
Islands of Desali
Deslalda
Desali's Capital
Petayrn
Nash
Senita
hite River
nt's Passage
Hydia's Capital
Harvester's stream
Cardinal River
uglauna

Chapter 1

The Shipwreck

"**W**hy did they do it?"

Prince Lerato could remember the night he asked that of his father. Lerato had been four years old at the time, yet the image of the burning ship drifting over the ocean was clear in his memory. He could remember alarm bells banging and horseback men galloping over cobblestone to provide aid at the shoreline. The ship was an orange ball of fire and light that reflected off the black water. The sleeping Capital of Hydia became dotted with lamps as the people awoke. Lerato recalled feeling confusion more than fear. At the age of four he had little reason to be afraid. He had watched the scene at a distance from a balcony. He had watched while standing next to his father, King of Hydia, and while standing within the safety of the fortress. Yet even as a boy he knew the ship had been attacked by the Kingdom of Desali, the kingdom of islands off Hydia's shore.

"Why did they do it?"

Lerato's father had been hunched over with his hands leaning on the balcony wall as he watched the scene. His face was in shadows from the night. Lerato could remember tugging on his father's sleeve.

"Father?"

"Because some men would rather rule an empty city than share a full one." His father had said that phrase many times since that day. Each time it was his way of explaining the Desalian's obsession for

Hydia's Capital and the series of attacks that have lasted for generations.

"Lerato, you must never trust a Desalian," his father had told him as they watched the burning ship. "Never."

Lerato was now older than his father had been on that day and he'd grown into the title of the 'reckless prince.' Lerato preferred the word 'trained,' unlike most of the royalty in Hydia's past who couldn't wield a blade. For that reason Lerato insisted he join his sister, the Princess as she sailed to the Hydian island of Senita. That was what brought him here, sitting in his assigned cabin with the lamps blown out.

He rubbed his eyes. The rhythmic rocking of the ship tempted him to sleep. Some would call it late in the night while others would call it very early in the morning. In either case, Lerato would stay awake through till dawn on a trek that came so close to Desalian territory. It had been nineteen years since the last Desalian attack, marking the Years of Silence, but every precaution had still been taken. They sailed with the most skilled and trusted crew and were guarded by twenty Hydian Knights and the General himself. They also departed at night with no announcement that the trip would take place. The precautions were enough to ease the mind of the Princess and let her sleep through the journey. Lerato couldn't.

Each flicker of lightning brightened the map spread across the table. The six islands were sketched on the parchment in careful cursive. Senita, the island closest to the southern edge of the map, continued to be the only island claimed by Hydia. The other five islands and the waters around them formed Desali. The image of the burning ship from his childhood haunted his memory.

A soft knock came to Lerato's door. In a way, he'd been expecting to hear from the General. The door only opened enough for someone to take one step inside.

General Kaytan's voice said, "A ship's been spotted."

"Desalian flag?" Lerato asked. The flag was rarely seen yet it seemed appropriate for it to be on a ship. The three waves of colour, blue, red, and black, stitched together on a block of cloth could send fear into any Hydian that saw it.

"It's too dark to tell."

No other Hydian ship would have reason to sail at this time of night. Aside from a Desalian, the alternative option was one of the unflagged cargo ships that claimed to trade between the various Hydian docks. Lerato took his cloak from the chair he'd been sitting on. As confident as he was in Kaytan's authority on the situation, Lerato wanted to be a part of it. He'd rather be on deck to witness the Years of Silence end than sit here and wait for reports about it.

On the deck, sailors were busily weaving among each other, adjusting ropes, and climbing the mast. The wind and rain whipped around them. General Kaytan led Lerato sharply to the right and up to where the ship's Captain was at wheel. Lerato could hear the Captain before he could see him. His voice belted orders over the storm and his gloved hands gripped the ship's wheel.

"We spotted 'er there, Sir," the Captain said to Lerato when he noticed him. He jerked his head to the side. "Port side. Shrinking in behind us."

Lerato squinted out over the ocean but, in the darkness, could barely make out the difference between the water and the clouds. Kaytan pointed, guiding Lerato's eye to a grey shadow.

"They've put out their lanterns," Kaytan said.

"Aye, they have," said the Captain with a glance back, "but we're outrunning 'em easily enough."

"If they're Desalian," Lerato said, "it may not be a planned attack."

There was a chance that this was an accidental crossing of paths. Lerato knew the thought was a hopeful one. He also hoped that the kingdom of Desali had enjoyed the peaceful years as much as the kingdom of Hydia had. Perhaps the Desalians had lost their obsession for Hydia's Capital. Perhaps they realized that after generations of fighting over land, few could remember what had started it all.

The Captain spun the wheel and the ship lurched to one side. He barked out an order for their own lanterns to be snuffed out. The dark shadow of another ship passed by in front of them. It's broad side towered over their bow and the Captain just managed to dodge a collision by swerving behind it. A series of thuds rippled across the deck. Kaytan pulled Lerato down by the shoulders and covered him until the rain of arrows had ceased. Two arrows struck the ground near them.

Kaytan stood just as quickly as he'd dropped. "Get more Knights on deck!" he ordered with a tone that a General deserved to have.

Lerato turned to look back at the original Desalian ship. As he did, his eye caught another thick shadow directly to their port side. In a moment the shadow took shape into a blunt bow. It was riding high on a wave and rushing down toward them.

"Captain! Another ship on the port side."

There was no time for the Captain to react. The side of the Desalian's bow struck the Hydian's stern. The impact knocked both Lerato and Kaytan off their feet. The two ships groaned against each other, creaking the wood. The Hydian ship leaned and veered to the side. White water swept onto the deck. Sailors were washed off their feet. At least two were already laying still with an arrow through them. When the two ships parted from each other, both were still upright. Lightning brightened the sky long enough to outline the three Desalian ships. The first was still in its original pursuit and gaining, the second had nearly redirected its course to follow close on the stern of the Hydian ship, and the third was also turning to do the same. Small dots of light appeared on each ship as they relit their lanterns.

The Captain pulled out a compass, muttered something to himself about what it read, and then stuffed it back in his pocket.

"How far off course are we?" Kaytan asked.

"We're due east."

That course would lead them through the Desali border.

The Captain glanced back at the vague shadows of the ships. "We won't be headed south again 'less we outrun 'em," he said. "They're not giving us room to."

"Do your sailors have weapons?" Kaytan asked.

"We're not a fighting ship, Sir."

This was where Lerato spoke up to add, "They're not trying to fight us."

"No disrespect to you, Sir," said the Captain, "but it's rare enough to meet one Desali ship. And three is more than I've ever seen at once."

"You're not expecting anything more?" Kaytan asked Lerato. There was consideration in his voice.

"Not yet," Lerato said. "Not until they've finished herding us into their own territory."

Kaytan nodded slowly. He looked out at the dots of light on board the Desalian ships. They were all close. "The first chance you have to reset our course, do it," he said to the Captain. "I'll keep my men ready but out of your way."

"Yes, sir."

Kaytan motioned for Lerato to follow as he headed down to the main deck. He stopped as he reached it. "They knew we were coming."

Lerato shook his head. "We took every precaution tonight."

"Then they heard the plans or noticed the preparation." Kaytan pointed to Lerato. "And they knew royalty would be on board."

"Aside from royalty, only a handful of men knew about this trip. Even the date wasn't decided until today."

Kaytan kept his voice hushed. "They didn't need to know the date, they just needed to know enough to be ready."

The words sparked a realization in Lerato. "What about Miken?"

Despite his father's warning, Miken was a Desalian man who Lerato knew well and had come to trust. At least, he had thought Miken could be trusted.

Kaytan paused at this. "You told him?"

"Not much, but he's smart enough to figure it out."

"You told him because of Alexria?"

Lerato winced at his own mistake. Alexria was Miken's wife and she was under Lerato's protection. That was the only reason she had come with them on this ship. He could feel his jaw tightening. "Because of her."

* * * * *

Alexria was thinking about him again. The way loud storms like these would frighten him. It would only take a few sharp rolls of thunder, maybe two or three, before she would hear his little feet pattering across the hall from his room to theirs. He'd stop at the doorframe and peer inside. Both Alexria and Miken would be awake by then, expecting the habit. Miken would be the one to climb out of bed and say, "Come on with Dad." He'd scoop up their four year old as though there was no weight to him. Miken held him close and the boy clung on. Miken would carry him to the archway that divided their room from the balcony and parted the heavy curtain just enough for them to see out. Alexria would watch them from her pillow, watch as each glow of lightning defined their precious silhouette, watch as the loud groans of thunder caused their son to bury his face further into Miken.

Their son. She'd been told that kind of loss, that kind of pain, would never really leave her. It was fifteen years later now. In that time Alexria had travelled all across the kingdom of Hydia many times, from the Capital on the shoreline to the river carving the western border to all the villages scattered between them. Still she couldn't escape the memories. She couldn't avoid the pictures that flared into her mind without warning. She'd become familiar with it, even come to accept it, but she couldn't stop it.

Alexria closed her eyes at the sound of more thunder. She found herself holding her necklace, the drop-shaped pendent between her thumb and little finger, a habit she's had as long as she can remember. She slowly let it go and took a long, deep breath. She wanted to do something. Something to occupy herself so she could tuck the memory away again. But she was on a ship now sailing from the Hydian Capital to the island of Senita. She wasn't a sailor. She could look after horses, look after a full household, and look after herself, but the consistent rocking of the ship on the ocean reminded her she was useless here.

Alexria opened the door to her small room as she heard footsteps approaching. Maybe she could find out how much longer they'd be sailing. Or maybe she could find something she could do.

The sailor passed by quickly. "Stay inside, miss. It's safer there," he said. He was drenched and dripping a trail of water down the length of the hall.

Alexria stood in the doorway and watched the sailor leave her behind. It was in moments like these when Alexria wished she were more like Miken. She wished she could put enough authority in her voice to demand what she wanted to know or learn how to do something here. She wished she could even enjoy travelling by ship the way he did. He told her once that the air, the mist, and the feeling of escape were what he looked forward to on his travels. He never mentioned storms. She never thought to ask.

The ship jerked as something smeared against its side. Alexria braced herself against the doorframe. That was more than a wave. It sent the sailor stumbling across the hall. Could it be a rock or a shallow part of ocean? Unless the storm forced them off course, the Captain should know to avoid such areas. Alexria paced back into her room, across the width, and then back out into the hall. She looked at the stairs. The answers would be above deck. Even if she just looked.

The ship lurched and sent Alexria flying forward, slamming into the cabin door across the hall. A rippling crack of wood engulfed the sound of the storm. Wood bending and snapping and beams ripping away from each other became all she could hear. She fell backwards, landing hard. She grasped for the doorframe of her room and pulled herself toward it. The sailor tumbled down the hallway like a barrel as he struggled to keep his feet under him. Alexria reached out as he stumbled past her but missed. The ship groaned. Cries and shouts came from all directions. Alexria clung to the doorframe with her body. The door swung open and closed against her shoulder. She tucked her head away from it. When everything ground to a stop, it didn't return to the swaying of the ocean waves. The ship was still. She expected to see or to feel water as the ocean tried to drown the ship. For a moment she remained clinging to the doorway, waiting. The rhythm of the storm and the ocean outside was all she could hear now.

A voice echoed in her memory. Miken's defeated voice. "I can't lose you, Alex. I can't lose you too."

Chapter 2

The Scar

15 years before the shipwreck

"...*The other Guardians of Hydia did not see them leave and, by the time they noticed, Alecan and Arimon were already half-way to the docks. The two men kept hidden from the patrols by following the shaded streets and moving through crowds.*" As Miken turned the page, he glanced up at where his son lay in bed. Though Laren's eyelids were heavy, he hadn't fallen asleep yet. The boy had learned early that the story would be set aside once his eyes closed. "*The two men agreed with the others that the plan was not the most wise. The chances of returning were low. The chances of success were even lower. Yet if they succeeded, the Desalians could finally be driven out of the Capital.*"

The story was interrupted by a knock on the door. Miken laid a piece of cloth across the page and closed the book.

"Can you keep going?" Laren asked. He kept his head on his pillow, probably too tired to lift it.

Laren's sickness had made him so pale and left deep circles under his eyes. He had been healthy only a few days ago. He had been running, smiling, and chattering away the way a four-year-old boy should. Now he couldn't leave the bed.

Miken set the book on the bedside table. "Just let me see who it is," he said.

"If it's Mum," Laren said when Miken was almost to the door, "could she visit?"

Miken wanted to say 'yes' to that sweet voice. But he had heard too many stories about how easily the sickness spread. It shouldn't have reached their quiet home in the countryside. Laren's fever hadn't set in until after Miken had returned from his trip to the islands. While he was there, Miken had spent days trying to avoid sick children and mourning parents. He would much rather be sick himself than see his son this way. Now he was too hesitant to go near either Alexria or their daughter.

"Once you're well she can," Miken said softly, hoping for the day.

He left before Laren could say anything more.

The servant waiting outside the door was Nevik. There was no urgency in his eyes, but there was enough concern to make his face hard.

"There's a man at the gate wanting to see you," Nevik said. "I don't recognize him."

"You told him I had no time?" Miken asked.

"I did, sir. But he strongly insisted." There was subtle emphasis on the word 'strongly.'

Whoever this man was, he knew how to get someone's attention. Miken knew enough about this man already to know he wasn't welcome.

"He says he brings news from the islands," Nevik said.

Miken had already guessed that much. "Which island?"

Nevik shook his head. "He didn't say. He only gave his name. Said it was Adicara."

"Adicara..." Miken said, testing the name and searching his memory. It wasn't familiar.

"He also wasn't shy about mentioning Desali," Nevik added.

Miken raised his eyebrows at this brave statement. In the kingdom of Hydia, Desalians were seen as dangerous spies plotting to overtake the kingdom. That was the narrow view of most common citizens. Miken knew better than that. He had dealt with enough Desalians to know he could hold his ground against one.

"If he laid a hand on you..." Miken began.

"No, sir," Nevik said quickly. "His threats were more... implied than direct. I know you never bring business inside the gates..."

"It's not worth dying over," Miken said. He patted Nevik's shoulder as he walked past. "I just hope he's as foolish as he is reckless."

* * * * *

A drizzle of rain pattered on the balcony as dusk was falling. Alexria closed the curtain to keep the breeze from chilling the room. By the time the curtain had been pulled across, the little one-year-old, Allia, had already crawled across the room to her feet.

The days had passed slowly since Laren had caught fever. Thankfully little Allia had kept her busy and distracted during that time. Her daughter plopped down on her bottom and reached up, making a squeal that hadn't yet formed into words. It brought a much needed smile to Alexria's face. She rested a hand on her rounded stomach where her third child waited to be born. She was told she couldn't afford to worry.

Alexria crouched down and lifted her daughter into her arms, cradling her close. Soon Allia would outgrow this, the way Laren had. Soon she would be walking, talking, and saying the most adorable phrases, the way Laren had.

Allia stretched her hand to Alexria's necklace, which hung just within her reach. On any other day Alexria would have hid the necklace under her tunic and out of her daughter's sight, but she needed the smile that it would bring them both.

Alexria undid her necklace and held the chain so the pendent dangled over her daughter. Allia took the drop-shaped pendent in her tiny fist. She seemed content just holding it, so Alexria let her. Alexria paced, rocking her daughter, humming a tune, and easing her to sleep.

Allia's brown eyes, much like Miken's eyes, slowly became heavy. Her hair was also much like Miken's, soft brown with a gentle curl at the ends.

A strange noise came from behind the curtain, like a squirrel had scurried across the windowsill. Alexria continued to rock her daughter to sleep as she watched the curtain sway in and out. The cloth played with the shadows. The pattering of rain played with her ears. She wanted to pull the curtain aside and look for herself but she couldn't bring herself to go near it. She couldn't explain why an odd fear had begun to stir in her stomach. The short scurrying sound came again and, this time, was followed by movement. As the curtains swayed out a cat-like creature crept out from underneath and into the room with slow steps. Alexria stepped back and held her daughter closer. Its back was arched and its hair was bristled up. Its thin, yellow eyes watched her as it moved. Its long, thick tail wisped back and forth. Its clawed feet moved toward her at a patient pace.

Then it all happened so fast, too fast for her to take in what was happening but vivid enough to stain her memory. First there came a rough hand. It grabbed her free wrist and wrenched it behind her back. Then, or maybe it was at the same time, a cloth was gripped over her mouth. Someone was behind her, a tall, strong stature that held her body to his. The cat creature crouched low and watched. A terrible stench came from the cloth on Alexria's mouth. She held Allia closer, thankful her daughter was asleep, then tried to shake herself from the man's grip. The rough hands tightened.

"Shh."

The whisper startled her enough to stop her.

"You don't want to wake the child," said the whisper.

Her daughter? What did he want with Allia? Alexria began to feel dizzy. She tried again to shake herself free but her effort was weak. She now felt the man supporting her more than she could support herself. The creature's tail moved back and forth. Where was Miken?

"If it assures you," he said as Alexria's world blurred, "I promise the child will die quickly."

Those were the last words she heard before her knees weakened and everything around her became black.

* * * * *

As Miken left the servant's house he was surprised to see the visitor's horse tied next to his own home. All the servant's knew better than to trust a stranger inside the gates, so the man must have let himself in and wandered through the courtyard. Enough rain had fallen to make the dirt courtyard squish under Miken's feet. Alexria must have closed her curtain because of the rain, blocking any chance of seeing her. He hadn't seen Alexria or Allia since last night when he had brought Laren to sleep in the servant's quarters.

As Miken neared the door to his home he returned his focus to the visitor. Opening the door brought a soft wave of heat. The visitor, Adicara, stood by the fireplace with his hands resting behind his back. A travelling cloak draped over his broad shoulders.

"You'll have to forgive me for taking shelter from the weather," Adicara said without turning. "It was a long ride from the Capital."

Miken left his boots on. "I don't talk business unless I'm on the islands."

An amused smirk slid onto Adicara's face as he looked at Miken. "Not enough rocks in the scenery here for you?"

"Not enough Desalians," Miken said plainly.

In the Kingdom of Hydia, Desalians were scattered and hidden to avoid arrest. The islands, however, were mostly Desali territory, thriving with families, strongholds, and men who dreamt of being kings. The islands were usually safest for business.

Adicara's smirk grew to a grin. "You'd be surprised how many Desalians are in the kingdom," he said, turning back toward the fire. "You have more friends than you realize."

"I doubt you're a friend," Miken said. "And I doubt I'll care about you're offer so I'd advise-"

"I'm here to warn you," Adicara said.

"I don't appreciate threats."

"Then you'd be best to pay attention now."

Adicara undid the tie of his cloak, lifted it from his shoulders, and draped it over the tall-backed, cushioned bench behind him. He had Miken's attention for the moment.

"There's a plague sweeping through the islands," Adicara said, "and has begun to make its way into the Hydian Capital. It moves fast and kills quickly. I'm sure you're heard of it."

"I've heard enough." Miken took slow steps across the room. The fire's heat strengthened as he neared it.

Adicara went on. "While some say it's no more than a plague, most rumours are calling it a strategic attack."

"Hydia wouldn't stoop to that level," Miken said.

"Desalians would."

Miken couldn't deny the argument. It was common for Desalian men in power to gain their titles with the help of a sword. Even the King, who Miken regretted to call his own brother, had used death and manipulation to reach that position.

Adicara went on. "Some men are blaming particular Dukes or Generals, some blame particular groups of commoners..." He paused with a breath. "And then there are those who blame the King."

The length of the cushioned bench was the only distance between them now and this is where Miken chose to stop. Adicara had steady eyes and a wide, solid stance, both of which Miken tried to match.

"I find it curious," Adicara added, "that the important men in Desali's Capital have remained nearly untouched by the plague."

Having been raised in Desali's Capital himself, 'nearly' was the word Miken wanted to object. "I'd know if the King had planned something like this."

Adicara shrugged and took a casual step forward. "Whether I believe you doesn't matter. Assumptions are just as dangerous as knowledge."

An uncomfortable knot began to swell within Miken's stomach. There was a threat layered within Adicara's words, something strangely vague but certainly present.

"Make your point," Miken said.

"You're clever enough to know by now why I'm here," Adicara said.

"Assumptions are dangerous," Miken said through a tight jaw.

Adicara's eyes smiled with pride. "Regards are sent to the King's family. However an unreasonable attack against their own allies is something that must be avenged. I'm told that royalty must feel the same pain felt by their people.

Miken was suddenly aware of the dagger at his own side and the lack of any obvious weapon on Adicara. Though he felt more alert by the fact that Adicara still had his hands settled behind his back.

"And why come all the way to me?" Miken asked.

Adicara let the question hover for a moment before he answered. "Vulnerable target."

That was enough of a clear threat for Miken to act on it. In one motion he drew his dagger and swept it toward Adicara's chest. To injure, not to kill. Not yet. Adicara blocked Miken's arm and made a swing of his own. Something hard struck Miken's cheek and he was given an extra shove into the back of the cushioned bench. The whole bench tipped and toppled over and Miken rolled onto the floor.

The most horrifying sound shrieked into the air then. It was the nearby cry of a baby. Allia's cry. But from where?

Adicara sprang over the fallen bench, his dagger flashing in the firelight. Miken rolled to his feet. He glanced over the room as he turned to face his opponent. The floor was bare. So was the stairway.

The pile of blankets by the window were still neatly folded. Where did Allia's cry come from? Miken brought his forearm to Adicara's to block the swing of his dagger. He then struck his fist hard into Adicara's ribs. Miken didn't have his own dagger. It was somewhere on the floor. Allia's cry came from the direction of the door. Adicara slammed a fist into Miken's side, knocked the dagger's hilt across his cheek, and then swept the dagger's blade. Miken dodged backwards but still felt a harsh scratch across his chest. Miken waved his arms to regain his balance. He planted one foot behind him and then kicked with the other, sending Adicara stumbling backwards.

There she was. On the ground beside the door, right where Miken had walked past, there was a blanket draped over a tall-handled basket.

Adicara was suddenly back upon him and Miken was stunned by a strike to his chin. Before Miken could recover, something solid pounded into the back of his head. Then black silence fell over him. Allia's crying stopped. The grunts and shuffling of the fight stopped. When Miken's eyes opened again the room was cold. The firelight was dim. The door was open. The basket where Allia had been was empty.

Miken jumped up, stumbled for a step, and ran out the door. Adicara's horse was gone. The gate was open to the black night outside the wall. Miken ran out through the gate. There was no distant sound of a gallop or sound of Allia. There was only the patter of the rain around him. The rest of the world was quiet and hiding the new enemy. Miken could feel his chest tighten.

"Adicara!" he shouted into the night. "You're a dead man, you hear me! I'll find you!" His voice echoed across the land. There was no sign of Adicara being close enough anymore. No tracks on the hard, softening ground. There was no sign of his daughter.

Steps ran up from behind him. Miken didn't turn.

"Sir," Nevik said. He was out of breath. "Alexria's in labour. The baby's coming."

Miken had to turn away from the empty land. He still had Alexria and Laren to protect. He couldn't find Allia tonight without risking his wife and his son. He knew he had to turn away. His eyes searched the shadows from where he stood. If only Allia were within reach. If only she were right there and he could catch a glimpse of movement to prove it. But only the wind swayed the crops and the grasses. He had to walk away. Miken forced himself to turn. Just walk away. He took one step toward the gate, still listening for the chance of a child's cry in the night. He took another step. He'd find Allia. He had to. Turning away from her now didn't mean he'd never search for her.

Miken walked through the gate and toward the house. By the time he was inside he could hear the familiar cries of Alexria giving birth and his walk became a run. When Laren and Allia had been born Miken had waited outside the room until it was over. But not this time. Not tonight.

Miken pushed open the door to the room. Yeles, the servant at Alexria's feet, didn't tell him to leave. Alexria's eyes were wet and defeated.

"Mike," she said at the sight of him.

Miken came to her side and took her hand in both of his. "I'm here now," he whispered. "It's alright."

"He took Allia."

"I know," Mike whispered.

She looked as though she would have gotten up if she could have. "We need to find her. We need to bring her back."

"I know." He brushed a strand of blond hair off her face. He slid closer to her. "Do this first, alright."

Her eyes swelled with water as he said it.

"Do this first." He couldn't bring himself to say anything more than that.

Alexria squeezed his hand. She let out a long groan of pain which turning into panting sobs. "I can't," she said, shaking her head. "I can't do it."

"Yes you can," Miken said gently. He kissed her temple. "You're strong, remember. I've always said that."

Alexria shook her head again. Tears escaped from her eyes and her mouth trembled. "The baby's too early."

Miken knew this. Alexria had only carried this child for two of the three seasons she needed to. It would be a still born. There was no use pretending otherwise. Miken could feel the reality of it choking him. He leaned his forehead against her temple so his lips were near her ear.

"I can't lose you, Alex. I can't lose you too."

* * * * *

When it was done, Alexria wept until the urge to sleep overcame the tears. Miken lay next to her and held her close. She woke when she felt Miken leaving the bed. He covered her shoulders with the blanket and closed the door behind him. He said nothing. Neither did she. She stared at the curtain swaying in and out. The new child had been still and quiet. Neither Alexria nor Miken held the child. They couldn't bring themselves to name it either. Their servant, Yeles, had simply taken the small bundle in her arms, laid it in a basket at her feet, and covered it with a white cloth. This child was gone. Allia was gone. And soon Laren would be taken from her by whatever the sickness was. Alexria closed her eyes and pulled the blanket tighter around herself. It wasn't fair. How could it be fair?

The door to the room slowly opened, bringing some light in with it. Alexria didn't lift her head and waited for Miken to come back to her.

"Mum?"

The small word stole Alexria's breath. She lifted herself up to see Miken coming in with Laren in his arms. Her son looked like a little angel, sweet and precious. It felt like so long since she had seen him. Miken carried him to the bed and Alexria sat up. She wanted to race to them both and wrap them in her arms but she feared that, if she did, if she moved too suddenly, or if she held too tight, then they would be swept away from her like in a dream. So she sat and waited and swallowed back her tears so her son wouldn't see them.

"We've been reading a story," Miken said. "We wondered if you'd like to join us."

Miken carefully sat Laren on the bed next to Alexria, leaning him against her open arm and shoulder. He was warm to sit next to. His tiny figure was so comforting.

"I'd love to," Alexria said. She kissed the top of his head and held her lips there for a long moment. His hair smelt like the lavender candles that must have been in his room.

"Why are you sad?" Laren asked.

A tear slipped from Alexria's eye as she heard this. She stoked his hair. He had such thick, playful hair. "I'm not," she said in a near whisper. "I've just missed you." She kissed his head again. "I've missed you so much."

Miken came into the bed and put his arm around Laren's back, as Alexria's was. He opened up the book where he had marked the page. "*Yet if they succeeded, the Desalians could finally be driven out of the Capital. And so they smuggled themselves onto the ship and set off across the ocean. The Capital and everything familiar to them slowly drifted further and further away, leaving them bound for places unknown.*"

Chapter 3

Crossing Borders

After the shipwreck

The scene on deck of the ship was enough to slow Alexria to a stop. When she'd first boarded at the Capital the ship had been dark but orderly. The sailors readied the ship and carried out their orders without question of what needed to be done. The Hydian Knights were coordinated as they took up their positions and escorted Alexria to her assigned cabin. But now, after the crash, the sailors and knights jostled about the deck like lost boys. Some were shouting at each other, some tended to the wounded, some tried to manage the ropes being flailed in the storm, some stood with their hands raked through their hair. Alexria hesitated. She didn't know where to start or what had happened. How could this have happened?

One of the nearby sailors came to her once he saw her. His face was different from most of the others. He was calm and controlled. He wore the bandana of either the Captain or the First Mate, but she couldn't remember what was meant by the green colour.

"Miss," he said, addressing her. "You'll be needin' weapons to be up here. You have some to use?"

Alexria had expected to be told to go back below deck where it was 'safer.' Instead she nodded. "They're in my cabin."

"Then you best fetch 'em." He turned to direct someone else.

"Sir?" Alexria asked quickly.

The man turned and extended an inviting hand. "The First Mate," he said and there was strength in his handshake.

"Yes. Sir... where are we?" Alexria forced out the foolish sounding words.

"Desalian territory."

Desali. How could she be there? It was the one place Miken begged her never to go and where he feared he couldn't protect her. It was the one place where Hydians rarely returned from.

"Miss," the First Mate said, stopping her thoughts from going further, "we'll be needin' your help."

Alexria went to her cabin before she could start thinking again. She needed to help. She could do that. She found her weapons scattered on the floor with her small bundle of belongings. She checked them over with a glance as she picked them up. Her sword, her bow, her quiver. Alexria counted the arrows in her quiver, walking her fingers from tail to tail. Fifteen. A good number for hunting or facing the occasional thief in Hydia, but would that be considered useful here?

If Miken were here, she'd be able to follow his lead. At the first mention of Desalian territory Miken would be listening to reports and advising strategies for defense. Alexria didn't have the authority to do that. Neither did Miken, but that never stopped him from doing what he needed to do.

An odd pattering sound caught her ear and she stiffened. It was like a gallop but lighter, faster. The steps were quick thuds and scratches, more like clawed paws than clicking hooves. She found herself looking to the door and above her, searching for the creature but finding nothing. It was like a dog or a cat. Alexria felt her stomach cringe at the thought of cat. When the sound fell silent, Alexria slung her quiver around her shoulder, took up her bow, and went back above deck into the rain.

The sailors and Hydian Knights seemed to be coordinating themselves a little more now. The First Mate stood in the middle of the deck, directing men and answering questions. Alexria started toward him to ask for a task. Commotion rose up. Shouts of warning and panic and blades being drawn. Alexria turned to see a cat-like creature leap toward the chest of a man and tear its claws across his flesh. The same creature she had seen all those years ago when her daughter was taken. An Etimire. She'd only ever seen one like this Etimire. And it meant Adicara was close.

* * * * *

After the Captain was killed in the crash, the First Mate was the first one to step into a commanding role and return order to the disoriented men. He assumed an authoritative presence that the men listened to and Lerato was impressed with. Satisfied that the main deck was in good hands, Lerato returned to his cabin. Princess Genev, his sister, was already there. She sat holding her shawl tightly around her shoulders as her husband, General Kaytan, was tying a bandage around her ankle. Of the three of them, Genev was the only one that hadn't been out in the storm and so she was the only one who wasn't dripping water on the floor.

"It's only a sprain. She'll be alright," Kaytan said as he finished with Genev's bandage.

"That's good." Lerato's weapons were piled on the table across the room. He pulled out the sword and eyed the long metal. Wooden sparing poles were what he trained with most often, but his experience with a sword was enough to make him comfortable with it. He sheathed it and tied it to his belt.

The ship had remained relatively intact, with the stern and port side receiving the most damage and the hull propped up on coastal rocks. They wouldn't be sailing again. Though the Desalian ships had disappeared from sight again, they were bound to return in search of survivors. In addition to that, the rocks they had crashed into were part of the Petayrn coastline. Petayrn was the smallest of the islands, but it was still part of the Desalian Kingdom.

"Lerato..." Kaytan said as he joined his side.

"Where will Genev be when the attack comes?" Lerato asked.

"She needs to get off the ship." His voice was surprisingly patient.

"Why?"

Kaytan leaned back against the table and folded his arms. "We have limited men, resources, and attack options."

Lerato raised his eyebrows. "We can't surrender this ship."

"I didn't say we would."

"We need *one* day." Lerato circled the table so he could see the map. "Our scout ship is scheduled to leave the Capital this morning at dawn. Once they realize we never reached Senita, we can have reinforcements here by tomorrow afternoon - maybe tomorrow morning."

"A day is a long time."

Lerato tapped the map as his mind raced through the defence options offered the by ship. The map's sketches were useless to him. He needed a map of Petayrn that defined the land and layout of the features. "We're sitting on the coastal rocks," he said. "There has to be some advantage to that."

Kaytan took a long breath and turned to face him. "We have until dawn. By then every man on this ship will be either killed or captive."

Dawn. That felt like no time at all.

Kaytan continued. "That is a fact you need to accept." He circled the table and stood next to Lerato. "If a crowd leaves the ship, the Desalians will hunt that crowd. If a crowd remains on board and only a few leave, those few should be able to leave unnoticed."

Genev was watching them with anxious eyes. She looked sweet and harmless, despite being only a few years younger. A battle was no place for her. A Desalian prison was no place for her either.

"Who's going with her?" Lerato asked.

"You are."

Lerato snapped his eyes back to Kaytan. "If my men are fighting, then so am I."

A frantic knock came to the door of their cabin and startled Genev.

Kaytan went to it with his attention on Lerato as he walked. "If your men are captured, you can't be," he said. "As long as we're outside the Capital, you're my responsibility. You both are."

Kaytan opened the door to the rain as Lerato returned his attention to the useless map. A cold air was quick to sweep in.

"Excuse me, sir, but there's a... a cat on board."

Lerato raised his eyebrows, amused. The young man at the door was drenched like everyone else on deck.

"A cat, sailor?" Kaytan asked.

The sailor shifted and searched for the right words to describe it. "The woman on board called it an Etimire." He said the word slowly as though he were recalling how to pronounce the word as he was speaking it.

"Alex said that?" Lerato asked. Aside from Genev, Alexria was the only other woman on this ship. He didn't want to say that Alexria had helped Miken plan this shipwreck. It was difficult to see her capable of such an accusation. Yet the subtle urge was there.

"I don't know her name, sir."

"Did she say what an Etimire was?"

As the sailor began to shake his head, Genev spoke up from where she sat at the side of the cabin.

"The creatures dwell in the forests beyond our Northern border," Genev said. Of everyone here, Genev would be the one to know, considering the library was her preferred place to be. "Stories describe them as vicious cats with no known predators to threaten them. Yet they exist more in stories than in Hydia. The Etimire have no reason to leave their forest, let alone to be on a ship."

"My apologies, my lady," the sailor said, "but if it had no reason to be here it wouldn't have killed a man already."

This caught Lerato's attention enough to start him toward the door. It could be heard outside when he paused long enough to listen through the rain. The shouts among the sailors and Knights were more than just coordinating and preparing defences. The shouts were urgent. The men were scrambling and, those Lerato could see, were looking up and around them.

"Where's the Etimire now?" Kaytan asked.

"It's climbed the main mast, sir." The sailor started back out onto the deck, leading the way.

Kaytan paused Lerato at the doorway with a raised hand. "How possible is it," Kaytan asked, "for there to be a Desalian Etimire?"

Lerato had hoped the cat was nothing more than a stowaway. That explanation was the only logical one. He hoped against the day Desalians learned to train the creatures. "It's certainly a new Desalian trick if I've ever seen one," he said.

Chapter 4

Royal Alliances

15 years before the shipwreck

Miken was too young to dig his son's grave. That was the job of an old man weathered and broken by the land. When he finished Alexria was waiting for him with saddle bags packed for the two of them. They left that morning. The servants said nothing of it. If anything they seemed to expect it, even helping to ready the horses and packing food. The three day journey only took two, but it passed by so slowly. All the while Miken knew he was heading to Desali. He needed to find Allia, Adicara, and whatever fool paid to have such a thing happen. But Alexria couldn't come. Desali wasn't a place for her. He couldn't protect her there. He couldn't protect Alexria if he left her behind either. She was in no state to look after herself considering she was more of a mess than he was. The only words she'd said to him were "We need to leave," and "Are you still awake?" Miken had nodded his response both times. Nothing more. When they slept, her arms were wrapped around herself instead of around him. He needed her arms around him, but he couldn't bring himself to ask.

So who would look after her when he left? Everyone he trusted was back within his own household. Everyone skilled enough to defend her was Desalian. And yet somehow Miken found himself entering a Hydian banquet hall in the Capital after requesting an audience with Prince Lerato and the High Lady. It seemed appropriate for royalty to protect the citizen's needing protection.

The last time Miken had met with either of them had been years ago, before he and Alexria had children. Miken had gotten tangled up with a Desalian attack on a Hydian banquet, resulting in his arrest. What had surprised him was that the High Lady of Hydia called for an audience with him. Not any of the other Desalians involved. Only he had been brought up with shackles on his wrists to her quarters in the royal halls.

The High Lady had become a legend among the kingdoms. Though Miken had seen her from a distance at various banquets, seeing her in person felt daunting. Not because of her appearance. Her simple gown, long white hair, and timeless face made her look quite harmless. Instead it was who she was that intimidated him. Of all the people in all the kingdoms, the High Lady was the only one to have lived for ten generations, spending her days guiding and advising the Hydian people. Her immortality was something Desalians dreamt of for themselves but had no way of claiming. As Miken entered her quarters, he assumed her importance was why Lerato had also been present and armed.

"You called for me, my lady," Miken said when the guard left him alone with Lerato and the High Lady.

"I did," the High Lady said with her gentle voice. "I believe your actions during the attack were misunderstood by the Hydian Knights."

That wasn't something Miken would argue. His attempt at sabotaging the attack had been mostly successful.

The High Lady remained seated on her long cushioned bench. "On occasion I am given authority to release a prisoner of my choosing," she said. "In light of this evening's events, I have chosen you. Should you accept my offer, your freedom and future actions will be a reflection of my choice."

It was the opposite of the penalty he was expecting to hear, making it feel like a test. Lerato remained at the side of the room with his arms folded across his chest. It didn't make sense for Hydians to release a known Desalian.

"Why me?" Miken asked.

"You differ from the others," the High Lady said.

"I disagree," Lerato said. His tone and cold stature suggested it. When Miken glanced to him Lerato added, "So you're aware where I stand."

The gaze of the High Lady was more welcoming. "Miken, my offer is not one to be taken with a light heart," she said gently. "I have chosen you for the potential I have seen in you. However potential remains in the hands of the one who holds it."

Despite being uncomfortable with how well she could read him, he trusted her word. It was Lerato, however, that didn't appear convinced.

"How do I know you won't send for my head the moment I leave?" Miken looked at Lerato after he finished his question.

Lerato held his strong gaze. "One of the last men she released became a Guardian of Hydia," he said.

Miken hadn't known this. "I doubt that man was Desalian," he said in challenge.

"He was," the High Lady said.

Miken glanced to her and then back to Lerato. Miken had known little of the Guardians of Hydia back then, and even later he had to look hard to confirm the fact. He'd found it hard to believe a Desalian could survive as a traitor to his own kingdom.

"I may not agree with her," Lerato added, "but I trust her insight."

"Miken," the High Lady said in her soft voice, "your fate is more than what others have decided for you. Regardless of your Desalian blood, your path is for you to choose."

"And if I accept your offer?" Miken asked, considering the possibility.

The words brought the small glow of a smile to the High Lady's face. "Lerato is here as a witness to your release and the promise of your freedom. You are free to come and go as you wish."

Now, years later, Miken doubted his face would even be recognized. In a way he hoped it wouldn't. Being a Desalian was best to keep hidden when in the Hydian fortress. He paced back and forth in the empty banquet hall, trying to occupy the long wait for his meeting. He hoped to request protection for Alexria and then leave before any situation could arise.

The wooden doors squealed open and Lerato walked in wearing formal Prince attire as though he were about to attend another important event. The High Lady hadn't come with him. Two Hydian Knights stood guard at the entrance.

Lerato stopped a stride away from the table and spread his arms out impatiently. "What do you want?"

The greeting wasn't the welcoming one he'd hoped for, but Miken continued anyway.

"Simply," Miken said in answer, "I'm here for a favour."

Lerato scoffed and turned to leave.

"It's for her, not for me," Miken said.

"And who's 'her,'" Lerato asked, turning back, but then his eyes wandered to the side of the room. He must not have noticed Alexria at first. She stood leaning against one of the pillars and looking out at the Capital's scenery. She had a hand on her necklace. Or rather, an identical necklace belonging to Allia, which had been set aside until their daughter was old enough to wear it.. Alexria's necklace had vanished that night along with Allia.

"I need you to look after her for five days," Miken said.

"Why? Because you can't?"

"I have things I need to do."

"And what kind of things does a *Desalian* need to do?"

Lerato's memory was better than Miken had hoped. When the guards did nothing in reaction to the word 'Desalian,' Miken assumed the High Lady's promise of freedom was being upheld.

"Important things," Miken said to Lerato.

Lerato thought for a moment and then asked, "How long have you been with her?"

Miken hated questions that tried to prove a point. He didn't have time for them. "It doesn't matter."

"And how many times have you left her before?"

"It doesn't matter."

"Then why come to me now?"

Miken didn't trust him that much. "Will you do it or not?"

Lerato didn't answer for a moment. He stood staring with his arms crossed and his brow creased.

Miken took a couple steps forward. He didn't know how much of the conversation had carried to where Alexria was at the end of the banquet hall. The nearby Knights would certainly be able to hear them.

When he spoke again, Miken lowered his voice and held back the urge to demand what he wanted. "I'm not asking you to trust me."

"Good."

Miken continued despite the comment. "And I'm not asking you to do this for me. But Alex ..." He motioned to her with the slight turn of his head. "She deserves to be safe."

Lerato remained quiet, keeping his thoughtful expression. But this time his gaze moved to Alexria. Miken couldn't tell what he was thinking, whether he was searching for reasons to agree to it or forming excuses for why he should walk away. He had every reason to walk away.

When Lerato spoke again he was more quiet and the challenging tone had left his voice. "Why are you asking *me*?" He didn't look back at Miken until after his question.

It was Miken's turn to take a long time to speak. He knew the answer. He knew that Lerato was one of the few men he was acquainted with who wasn't Desalian, making him the only man he could trust with Alexria's safety. But knowing it and saying it were two different things. He'd look too weak if he did that.

"If you plan to waste our time -," Miken began.

But Lerato was quick to interrupt him. "I plan to help you. And I plan to trust *her.*"

"Then we have an agreement?" The sooner Miken could get him to agree, the less likely Lerato would change his mind. The Prince was said to be honourable that way.

Lerato glanced to Alexria, stared hard at Miken for a moment, then nodded. "It seems we do."

* * * * *

Navigating the maze of staircases in the Hydian fortress was instinct for Lerato. All the ups, downs, splits, and merges were logical after a childhood here. So when Lerato found himself arriving at the High Gardens instead of the Royal halls, he knew his mind was distracted. He sighed and turned back toward the steps he had just climbed. The Royal halls were on the opposite side of the wide, hollow centre of the fortress tower. He would have to descend these stairs and climb a separate set in order to get there. Lerato leaned his hands on the stone railing instead. Perhaps taking a chance to pause was best for him.

The open roof above the hollow centre displayed a rich blue of an evening sky, explaining why the surrounding stairways and terraces were dimming. A torch was lit in a terrace at the base of the tower, six levels beneath him. The servants must have begun making their evening rounds. A few shadows of movement strolled the stairs and terraces beneath him. Aside from that, the evening was dull. There were no meetings, banquets, or assembly's to attend. He had already had dinner, which his sister had been late to and his father had commented on how much unnecessary time she spends in the library. He had completed his daily swordsmanship training, discussed military updates, walked the Northgate Gardens over lunch with his wife, and he even took time in the libraries to update himself on various histories. Lerato had intended to recline in his quarters for the remainder of the evening until he found himself here instead.

Yet what had been hanging in his mind all day, and keeping him distracted was Alexria. Lerato had expected the strong and demanding tone that he had heard from Miken, but what surprised him was hearing the subtle desperate plea that seemed contradicting. So why did Alexria matter so much to Miken? Lerato had always imagined the Desalians to be too cold to care about anyone or to feel anything. But what did that mean for Alexria? Lerato couldn't treat her like a Desalian when she didn't carry the same typical arrogance. She didn't even raise her eyes to him.

Lerato's wife, Lacina, had advised him to talk to her, saying the mystery of who she was would haunt him until he solved it. He found 'mystery' to be too important of a word. Yet now he found himself heading toward the conversation he'd been avoiding.

Alexria had been assigned guest quarters on the second level of the fortress tower. The guard assigned to her, as Lerato promised there would be, was posted in the hall outside her door. Lerato was greeted as "Sir" as he approached.

"I should say, Sir," the guard said, "she's not a usual guest."

"No?" Lerato didn't know why that surprised him.

"No, Sir. Most guests would take some time to explore the fortress. For her, I'd gamble she hasn't left her bed."

"Is she sick?"

"By her word she's not," the guard said. "And if it weren't for the food I wouldn't concern you with any of this."

"She's eating too much?" Lerato asked, assuming she followed the common pattern of guests over-enjoying the hospitality.

The guard's voice lowered with his answer. "Quite the opposite, Sir," he said. "She's barely eaten in the two days she's been here."

Something about that left Lerato unsettled. He nodded slowly and thanked the guard. Lerato knocked on the door to Alexria's guest's quarters and waited a long moment for an answer. None came.

The unsettled feeling still lingered in his stomach. Perhaps it was worry for her. Enough worry that Lerato opened the door himself.

Torchlight from the hallway streamed into the dark living room. The room was dressed typically for a guest's quarters. A table was against one wall holding a decorative water basin and lamps. A well cushioned bench was against the other wall. The bedroom, which he could see through the wide archway, was a little brighter but still dim. As he approached he could see that the curtains were open to bring in at least some light from the evening. There was the lump of a figure on the bed that he assumed to be Alexria. Waking her was not something he was prepared to do, nor did he feel it appropriate for a Prince, so he turned to leave. He'd have the guard report in the morning when she awoke.

"Did Mike come back early?"

Lerato turned back to the room. Alexria hadn't stirred but the voice had certainly come from her direction.

"No, he didn't," he said. "I didn't mean to disturb you."

She gave no response. The room was still.

"Do you need me to send for him?" Lerato asked.

There was a short pause. "It's not worth the risk for you," she said. "Or for Mike."

There it was again. Mike. The same way he called her Alex. Her words sparked more of Lerato's curiosity, but it was her quiet voice that stopped him from asking more. Defeated was the word he wanted to use, though he couldn't be sure. It was too dark to see her face or read her expression.

"Could I invite you to a walk?" Lerato asked. Maybe he could get some food into her too.

"Is that an order, my lord?"

Lerato couldn't remember ever being addressed by 'my lord.' "No, it's a request," he said as gently as he could.

There was finally movement in the bed as Alexria sat up. She wore the same clothes he had seen her in two days ago and they were creased enough for her to have been wearing them that long. She took her travelling cloak from a nearby chair and wrapped it around herself like a housecoat. As they left the room Lerato assured the guard that he'd return her in good time.

For the long stretch of hallway they walked in silence. If there was to be a conversation, Alexria wasn't about to start it.

"When were you last in the Capital?" Lerato asked. The question felt forced.

"Five years ago," she said.

"Five years...? Then you'd have been here when... when Desali attacked the Civilian Festival." Lerato almost said 'when Miken was arrested,' but that likely would have raised more of an unpleasant memory.

Alexria stared blankly ahead as though she were recalling the moment. "I helped Mike defend against the attack."

"You did?" Lerato had forgotten that any woman had helped in the defence. The memory for himself was little more than a blur of movement and blades and the pounding of his heart in his ears. "Then you must have some skill with a blade," he said.

She shook her head and looked down at the steps they began climbing. "That was a long time ago," she said. Then, in a near whisper, she added, "Things would be different if I still could."

Lerato wished she would say more. Even something about where she learned to fight or why she chose to stop. Did Miken have anything to do with it? He wished she would answer the questions that he didn't know how to ask. If Samila were here, she would know. Despite being the High Lady, her gentle nature could reach to the heart of any common citizen. Yet while Lerato thought this was something he could also do, the stairs seemed to linger as long as the silence did.

Alexria came to a sudden stop. "I should go. I have... things I need to do." Her eyes darted across the stone of the floor, railing, and walls.

Lerato was on the step above her, having not stopped as quickly. "I can send someone to aid you if you'd like."

"No. No." She rubbed her forehead and shifted on her feet. "I need to do it. I just... It's important." She paused, moving her mouth as though she wanted to say something but couldn't find the words. "I should go." With that she spun, making her cloak fan out behind her, and started back toward her room.

"Alexria, wait."

Yet her quick steps didn't slow. Lerato had to trot down the steps to catch up to her and block her path with his arm to stop her. She said nothing and kept her eyes downcast. The corners of her mouth trembled as though she approached tears. What had he done wrong? How could he have broken her so quickly? Lerato lowered his arm, freeing her path again. Alexria hesitated for a short moment, then continued down the stairway. She didn't look back and she made no sound except for the tapping of her steps on the stone. Lerato watched her as long as she was in his view. He watched her hug her arms around herself as she went. He watched her strides lengthen as she reached the hallway at the bottom of the stairs.

Perhaps he wasn't the one to break her. Considering she had spent the last two days alone in her quarters, the assumption felt appropriate. Yet if she was already broken, what had happened to make her that way?

* * * * *

When Miken sailed to Desali, he would usually visit only two or three islands at a time. As the Ambassador of the King to the Desalian people, he only needed to report on the updated strength and situation of the various Desalian strongholds. He never spent more time than he needed to and there was usually little to report on.

Yet when he set sail from the Hydian coast this time, he wasn't going to fulfill any orders. This time he went to all five islands. This time he went with his memory focused on the image of Adicara's face. The man's dark eyes gleamed with sickening confidence. Miken looked for those eyes in every face he saw at the Hydian docks, on the ship he boarded, and on the shore of the island of Emyl. It was on Emyl in the village outside the fortress that Miken saw a young child. He didn't know why the child caught his eye. She was much more steady on her feet than Allia was. The Duke of Emyl had a ten-year-old daughter, with hair darker than what Allia's would be at that age, and a young son, who was said to be sick in bed the way Laren had been. Adicara was nowhere, though the Duke noted that the name sounded somewhat familiar.

The pattern continued through the islands. Adicara was a name, almost a rumor, but little more than that. Even on Miken's own island of Deslalda the King had only heard of the name but had never met him. It was as if the man barely existed. Either that or he was the newest assassin and his work wasn't known yet.

Then there were the children. Miken didn't know there were so many in the island villages and fortresses. They never drew his eye before. Yet now he was haunted by it. Children running and crawling around the village houses, women rocking bundles of cloth, and young Desalians learning from Dukes, Generals, and Captains. Miken claimed to be tracking the progress of the plague and used that to see the faces of as many children as he could. The Duke of Nolak had five sons, three of which were ill. The Duke of Nash had a daughter and a son and had recently lost his youngest son. The Duke of Petayrn had young twin boys, both sick, and a pregnant Duchess. On Deslalda, the Desalian King claimed to be untouched by the plague, but wouldn't let anyone near his four children for fear that the sickness would spread to them. It was the Generals and Captains of Deslalda, however, that seemed to be suffering from the plague's blow. Miken didn't see Allia among any of them. He'd even looked at the faces of the young girls, just to be sure.

When Miken returned to the Hydian Capital on the morning of the fifth day, he turned to walk along the docks instead of going to Alexria in the fortress. He wove through the mess of sailors and merchants and other workers. When he reached the end of the wooden docks, he continued on over the rough, rocky shoreline. The bustle of the crowds was replaced by the steady beat of the waves. Miken didn't sit until the crowds were too far behind him for him to hear. The rock he sat on was flat and cold. At least the wind wasn't harsh. The sun had barely risen out of the ocean horizon and it streamed into Miken's eyes. He looked at his feet instead. He pulled the knife out from the side of his boot and spun it around in his hand. His wrist and fingers moved out of habit to spin the knife up, to the side, the other side, around, down, and back up again. The metal flashed in the sunlight.

What would he say to Alexria when he reached her. He didn't miss home. It wasn't good to be back. There were no children to ask about. Miken closed his eyes while he kept the knife spinning. There were no children. There wouldn't be any more children. He could see that in Alexria's eyes and he was sure it was in his own eyes as well. Neither of them had the heart to do it again. So where did that leave them? They had a farm and land, but neither of them cared about it. It was food to eat and sell. It was a place for their family to be raised. It was far enough from the Capital to be safe. It was supposed to be safe.

Miken opened his eyes to the knife again. What was there to go back to? What good was he to Alexria? The knife was a fluid of movement. Spinning and flashing. Swiping and gleaming. Cool, sharp metal. Certain. Useful. Effective.

"Mornin', sir."

The voice startled him and Miken stopped the knife's motion with a swift grip. It was a harmless looking man carrying a wooden bucket in one hand and a fishing pole in the other. His plain clothes said he wasn't rich, but he didn't look overly poor either. He walked over the rocks toward Miken and toward the docks. Miken tucked away the knife.

"She'll be a fine mornin', wouldn't ya say?" the fisherman asked.

The sun was still glaring in Miken's eyes. "It'd help if I could see it."

The man grinned. "Fair enough. Fair enough. At least the hills and the city won't blind you." He waved his arm toward the land at Miken's back.

As the fisherman approached, he paused as though he were going to stop for more conversation.

"You should keep walking," Miken said.

The man nodded as though he had taken no offense. "No worries at all."

He took his time, though, as he manoeuvred his footing over the rocks and toward the Capital. After he'd passed by Miken he stopped and took a step back. Miken considered drawing his knife again to strengthen his advice.

"You don't have to take it with you," he said, reaching into his bucket, "but I caught a few extra this mornin'." He pulled out a small, limp fish and laid it on the rocks near Miken. He grinned. "Fresh from the sea."

Without waiting for any thanks or rejection, the fisherman turned and continued on along the shore. Miken watched him for a long time, expecting him to turn around again or to even make a glance back. He seemed like the type that would wave an additional good-bye from a distance. Yet when the man reached the wooden docks he carried on as though this were his typical good morning.

He was right about the city. Even looking at the docks, with the sun beside him, wasn't as blinding as looking out over the water. The city was a rough pattern of sun and shadows. The fortress stretched up above it all and the sun gleamed white on the stone. Alexria would be waiting for him there. He always came home on time. There would be no children now. But there would be her. Miken stood. His legs were stiff. His eyes were heavy from little sleep. His last five days were wasted with nothing to show of them. The least he could do is go back to her. Miken began his walk along the shore and back to the Hydian fortress. He left the fish behind him on the rock.

* * * * *

Alexria was sure she used to look forward to Miken returning from the islands. He would always tell her how long he'd be gone, always give her a number of days to count down. She could remember looking down the road countless times on that last day and could remember smiling when she finally saw him. But whatever feeling she used to have when she'd first see him, whatever joy or relief or excitement or whatever she felt... she couldn't bring herself to feel it now. It was a long five day wait for him this time, which was less time than he was typically gone for. Now Miken stood in the doorway of the guest quarter's bedroom, arriving on time as he always did. Seeing him made Alexria feel even more heavy. She didn't get out of bed. He didn't come past the doorway.

"You ready to go home?" he asked. His voice was quiet.

Home. To the fields Alexria had walked beside on the clear spring mornings. To the fireplace where she would tell Laren a story each night. To the hallway she would pace as she rocked Allia to sleep. To the courtyard and the crib and children's room.

"Alex?" Miken's voice was still quiet. "We can be home by tomorrow evening if we leave soon."

Alexria closed her eyes. "I can't go back."

Miken was quiet for a long time. The only sound was the soft breath of the wind swaying the curtains. When Alexria opened her eyes again, he was still in the doorway.

"We have to go somewhere," he said.

Alexria sat up and held the blanket around her shoulders. "Then let's go somewhere. Or everywhere - it doesn't matter. Or stay here."

"And do what?"

Alexria shook her head as her mind raced for an answer. She hadn't thought that far ahead.

"I know you're scared to go back," he said.

"I'm not -"

"Just-" Miken winced at the strength of his own voice. He paused as though to compose himself and, when he began again, his tone had settled back down. "Just let me finish," he said. "You have every right to be scared. And I know home doesn't feel safe but it's more safe than any road at night or a village we don't know or people we can't trust."

"Then teach me to fight." The words had come on their own but Alexria had been thinking them since her talk with Lerato. She shrugged helplessly. "I've already lost everything. So what should I be afraid to lose?"

Miken said nothing to this, but even from across the room she could notice the heavy rise and fall of his chest. She stood, leaving the blanket behind and facing the chill of the air. The walk to Miken felt long in the silence and she stopped a step away from him.

"Teach me to fight," she said in a whisper.

"I'm the wrong one to ask."

"You're the only one to ask."

He searched her eyes for another long moment and she held his fragile gaze.

He finally nodded and glanced to the floor. "I won't teach you to kill," he said. "That's my burden, not yours."

Chapter 5

First Arrows

After the shipwreck

The Etimire had aimed for the Knight's neck. There was a deep gash across the man 's collarbone. Alexria was kneeling in front of him with a torn cloth pressed against the wound. With her other hand she pressed cloth against a second, deeper gash across his side and chest. Every few moment's she'd glance up at the main mast to be sure that the Etimire was still there. The man's chest panted up and down and he coughed and wheezed. The rain whipped down at them. The man kept saying that he couldn't breathe and that it was getting worse. Alexria kept telling him to breathe slower and that he'd be alright. Even she didn't believe that. Another Knight asked what she needed. She shook her head and asked for more bandages, but by that time the injured man was already coughing up blood. His breaths shortened and laboured. His coughs became chokes and gasps. Then nothing. After a last, struggled gasp in, he let all of it out as his body sunk back against the wall. His chest stopped heaving. His eyes stared ahead of him with an empty gaze. Alexria could feel her own hands begin to tremble. She felt his neck for some sign of life, any sign of life.

"Alex?" It was Lerato's voice.

She could hear the men being coordinated by the General to have arrows ready on their strings and swords waiting in their hilts.

Alexria reached out an unsteady hand and closed the eyes of the man she tended to. She dropped the bandages in a wet slop on the deck. A hand touched her shoulder and in a flinch she shrugged it off her.

"Are you alright?" It was Lerato again, standing next to her now.

Alexria nodded. What had she done wrong? She'd saved men and women and children before. She'd helped them recover from their injuries. Why couldn't she save this man? The man's face was pale with rain dripping down it like tears. She felt numb. Her hands numb from the rain, her body numb from the wind, her heart numb of emotion.

Lerato crouched next to her in a way that he could face both her and the Etimire. "Alex," he said slowly, "I'm only asking you this because I have to. It's for the safety of everyone on board."

Pain and fear were creased in the dead man's face. He'd gasped for life. Fought a losing battle for it. Her son's face had been peaceful the morning he didn't wake up. Her little boy had been pale and cold and stiff, but at peace.

Lerato paused and shifted. "I need to know if Miken planned this attack. Or how likely it is that he did."

Miken had blamed himself when they lost their children. He'd never said it. Not in all these years. But she'd seen the weight of it on him, the burden that had been too heavy for him to lift off himself.

"Alex," Lerato said, bringing her thoughts back to the ship and the rain and the man still lying in front of her. "I need to know what you know."

Alexria stood. She had to get the scene out of her head. She opened her hands to let the rain wash the blood off. Lerato wiped them off with the corner of his traveling cloak. The thick cloth was damp.

"Alex, look at me." And when she did, he said, "Where's Miken?"

Alexria shook her head and took her hands back. "He wouldn't do this."

The Etimire scurried back and forth among the masts and crossbeams and lines. The dark outline of it leapt and climbed as its claws dug into the wood.

Lerato continued. "He's the only one who knew we'd be here. He had the time to coordinate this kind of attack." He kept his voice gentle. It seemed to take effort to.

Alexria watched the Etimire. She could picture that same outline, fifteen years ago, climbing its way to her windowsill before slinking out from beneath the curtain. Those claws and arched figure had caught her with fear that night. But not now. She wouldn't let Adicara and his Etimire intimidate her this time.

Lerato added, "Miken's the best explanation."

"You know him better than that." Alexria reached for her nearby bow and drew an arrow.

"Do I?"

She turned her attention from the Etimire for a moment so she could look at him. There was urgency, maybe even some panic in his eyes. He was searching for answers that she couldn't solve herself.

"You know Mike better than you think," she said.

Alexria returned her attention to the threat at hand. If it was her choice, the cat wasn't going to kill anyone else. The Etimire was darting over the crossbeam, dodging arrows and weaving ropes. Alexria kept her arrow steady. Of all the shots aimed up at it, it still looked unharmed. The target was too small and too distant. Instead there were more holes pecked into the sail. The Etimire slid along one of the ropes toward the mast. Alexria released an arrow toward one end of the rope, hoping to cut it and cause the Etimire to fall, but the wind tossed the arrow off its course. The rope was an even smaller target anyway. So what did she aim for instead? How could she protect these men?

The Etimire continued to run back and forth and side to side. Never down. Never toward anyone. It drew every eye, of the thirty-five maybe forty men, to stare up at the masts in fear. Was no one keeping watch elsewhere? They were sitting stranded on the shore of Desalian land, according to what she'd been told. She could see only a blurred shadow where the island would be and tiny specks of what could be lights. The churning waves and blowing storm drowned out any chance of hearing approaching footsteps. She walked closer to the edge of the ship, ignoring the Etimire for a moment. If the cat made any advances, she'd hear the alarm of the other men. The night was still so dark beyond the ship. How would they have warning of a coming attack if they couldn't even see the place they were coming from? There were only jagged clusters and stretches of what seemed to be shoreline rock.

Was there movement? Alexria couldn't be sure if she really saw it or not. The wind blew in strong gusts at a time. But, in the breath of time between them when the wind was still and the rain was streaming down instead of misting across, her view became a little clearer. The outline of the rocks became definite shapes instead of blurred shadows. Alexria strained her eyes. There it was again. Slow movement in and out of her view. Something. Or - as the shape became clearer - someone. A Desalian. Coming closer. Alexria wanted to glance across the deck to see if anyone else had noticed him, but she feared that if she looked away it would take too long to find his silhouette among the shadows again.

Alexria adjusted her grip on the bow. Despite her numbing fingers, it felt comfortable. The Desalian was still a good distance away. Maybe fifty strides if the distance had been over flat land.

Someone grabbed her and pulled her to the side and toward the ground. She heard a muffled "Look out" and then groan of pain. It was Lerato that grabbed her. Alexria caught a glimpse of the Etimire racing across the railing where she'd been and a sailor swing a sword toward it. Then, without effort, the Etimire was back up the mast and out of reach. Lerato slammed a frustrated hand against the deck as he lifted himself up.

"Are you alright?" Alexria asked.

"Just a graze," Lerato said in a stiff voice.

She was sure he was hiding pain from the injury she assumed to be on his back. She wanted to tend to it, felt it was her place to, but there wasn't time. She nodded her satisfaction with his answer and then looked back out over the railing. It was a long moment before she could find the Desalian in the shadows again.

"What do you see?" Lerato asked with his same stiff voice.

"Watch for the Etimire," Alexria said. Her bow and arrow were still in her hands. The closer the Desalian crept the easier it became to see him. Her thumb brushed over the arch of the arrow's tail. She listened to the wind, feeling the rhythm of gusts and silences, feeling the timing. She fitted the arrow to the string, twisting her fingers into the familiar grip. As the wind blew her hair beside her Alexria raised her bow, pulled the string back toward her ear, and readied her aim. She waited. The sound of her name came faintly to her ears but she didn't waver. The rain rippled across her view. Then the wind dropped to nothing. Her grip released. The arrow shot forward. The silhouette twisted as though his shoulder had been shoved and then he stumbled to regain his footing.

She heard a sword slide from its sheath. The commotion on the deck had become more panicked.

"Alex, get down," Lerato's voice was close to her.

Alexria tucked her bow close and ducked low. Lerato swept his sword low and wide across the deck. Then he swept it up high. The dark blur of the Etimire pounced over Alexria's head and over the ship's railing. Lerato's sword followed. A screeching scream echoed in the night as the Etimire fell overboard. The claws that had been tearing at flesh could now be heard scratching at the ship's wood. Lethal claws, like daggers. They had come too close to her.

"Is it gone?" a nearby sailor asked.

"For now," Alexria said. It would take more than a short fall to kill it.

"What did you see out there?" Lerato asked. His sword was ready in one hand. His other hand leaned on the railing.

"A Desalian," she said. "Just one."

"Another," General Kaytan shouted, pointing somewhere else in the darkness. "There!"

Alexria stood to look. Someone else on board the ship released the arrow that struck the second Desalian. There now seemed to be movement all over the rocky shoreline.

"Knights, arm your bows," the General ordered. "Sailors, keep watch for the cat. Eye every side and corner."

Arrows hissed from the Hydian ship into the shadows. Some struck their targets, others were tossed in the wind. Alexria strung another arrow to her bow to join the defense. She struck two Desalians before the shoreline rocks became still again. General Kaytan shouted orders to hold aim and keep watch, but it seemed that the group of Desalians that had been coming over the rocks had only been a small scouting party. The storm likely didn't allow much more of an attack to be made.

* * * * *

When the arrows started flying, Lerato took a step back from the railing to make room for the Knights. His back ached and complained at him. He glanced to the dead man who still lay off to the side. His own wound was only a graze. Lerato repeated those words in his mind. He could manage a graze.

Lerato stood next to Kaytan to watch, wait, and wish he could get a Desalian within reach of his sword. At least he had gotten a swipe at the Etimire and forced it off the ship. He'd hoped to see blood on his blade, yet he found it clean and wet with only rain. When the Desalian shore became still and Kaytan ordered his men to keep watch, Kaytan motioned for Lerato to take a step aside with him.

"If you're going to leave, it needs to be soon," Kaytan said. "Especially with your injury." He said the words quietly to keep others from hearing.

'Injury' was hardly the word Lerato wanted to use. Besides, leaving in this weather made the suggestion even less inviting. It'd probably break Genev as much as a battle would. "We've been successful so far," Lerato said.

"It'll only get worse."

"We'll hold them off."

"The cat was a distraction," Kaytan said in an impatient hiss. "The Desalians were scouts. When the attack comes, it *will* come. And there'll be no leaving after that."

It wasn't like Kaytan to lose his patience, much less to Lerato. Lerato blinked at it. Perhaps considering the option was something he could afford. It didn't mean he would have to.

"*If* we left," Lerato said, "what would we do after that?"

"You would flag down whatever rescue Hydia sends after us," Kaytan said. "You'll have to stay hidden for at least a full day until then."

A day of hiding and keeping his sword sheathed wasn't appealing. This was especially so when his men would soon be fighting a Desalian battle. Every available Hydian would be needed whether 'grazed' or not.

Kaytan took a step forward, bringing himself close, and lowered his voice. "My wife is on board," he said. "Your sister. If I could leave with her myself I would, but I can't. It's my duty to lead my men. It's your duty to keep the royal family safe."

If Lacina, his own wife, had been here, Lerato wouldn't have hesitated to leave. He wouldn't have trusted anyone else with her safety. Lerato sighed. "It seems we each have what the other man wants," he said, "but I'll do it."

This helped relax Kaytan's stature. He nodded his thanks.

As Lerato looked over the Hydian men, arrows stringed and watching, his eye noticed Alexria. She stood steady in the rain like all the others. Her posture was straight and definite like that of a trained archer. Her long hair was tossed in the storm's wind. She was also his responsibility. That was the only reason she was here. Yet seeing her reminded her of Miken.

"Would you trust Alexria to come with us?" Lerato asked.

Kaytan looked at her for a long moment. "Would *you*?"

"I thought I trusted her husband," Lerato said, "yet that was before we crashed here."

"But do you trust *her*?"

That was the question, wasn't it? As much as Lerato was tempted to say no, he was reminded of the man killed by the Etimire. The sight of death had almost been too much for her, despite the fact that she had recovered quickly from it.

"She's not Desalian," Lerato said. "I'd been surprised if she's ever really killed before."

Kaytan nodded. "She won't slow you down. If anything she'll defend you as well as you'll defend her. You may need that." He studied her for another long moment and then said, "Tell her she's coming with you, but make sure no one else knows of it."

Chapter 6

Circumstances

14 years before the shipwreck

Just as Lerato was about to knock on the door again, it finally swung open. Kaytan emerged from his dim quarters.

"I swear you wake me earlier every morning," Kaytan said, rubbing his eyes. His voice was thick from a night of sleep.

Lerato gave him a friendly slap on the shoulder. "It's good for you."

Kaytan grunted in response. The routine of sparring in the mornings was something they began several years ago. With Kaytan's duties as Captain of the Hydian Guards and Lerato's duties as Prince, the morning held the least busy moments of their day. Kaytan rubbed the sleep from his eyes and stretched his limbs.

The two men began with a stiff jog down the wide halls and, for now, a quick walk down each staircase. They wound their familiar route through the fortress until they approached the Western Gates. The air was cool in the shadow of the fortress tower. Lerato climbed the steep steps two at a time to the top of the fortress wall. Kaytan followed close behind. From there they turned to circle the long way around the wall instead of heading directly for the training arena. It added about another two thousand strides to their run, yet Kaytan said he couldn't begin sparring until he was awake. The circle around the fortress wall had at first been his suggestion, but it became a routine that Lerato had also come to appreciate.

With a cloudless morning, there was a definite line between where the fortress' shadow ended and the daylight began. As they reached the southwest corner and turned east, the view of the Hydian Capital revealed itself with each step. The sky was pale and bright with the bold streak of the sun sitting on the ocean horizon. Between the shoreline and where Lerato was in the fortress were clusters of buildings divided by streets. The view of rooftops looked as jagged as weathered rocks, yet the view was home for him.

Lerato and Kaytan continued their trek around the fortress wall. At the Northern Gate, they descended a set of stairs and weaved through the fortress again to reach the training arena in the northwest corner. They could already hear the clatter of wooden sparing poles slapping together. It wasn't often that someone reached the sparing arena before them, with the exception of the guard on duty.

"Morning, sirs," the guard said as they approached.

Lerato nodded his greeting. His focus was on the lone sparing match in the arena. From a distance, the two figures had seemed somewhat familiar. Now as he stood next to the guard's post at the arena's entrance, he was sure it was Miken and Alexria. The torchlight gave an odd glow to their match, but that wasn't what concerned him. There was heat in each swing of their poles. There was more heat than he'd expect to see in a training routine, as if there was some frustration or pain underneath each motion. It showed in their stern faces and blunt swings. Yet after a year of seeing Alexria weighted under some mysterious burden, it wasn't her that surprised him. It was Miken. If Miken knew anything he'd know not to encourage this kind of match. Nothing ever came from fighting through frustration. That was something the High Lady, Lady Samila, had told Lerato once. What Alexria needed was to talk and sort through whatever she had buried. Miken wasn't helping her.

"How long have they been here?" Kaytan asked.

"My duty began at daybreak," the guard said. "By then they were already here."

Kaytan nodded the way he did when he was thinking. He'd be assessing the situation, as he often did. He'd notice that Miken was the better swordsman. Though Miken's movements were quick, they were neither rushed nor offensive.

"Do you recognize them?" Kaytan asked.

"Is she not the woman put under your care each season?" the guard asked with a glance to Lerato.

"It is."

Either Miken or Alexria must have found work somewhere inside the fortress. That was the most common way to receive living quarters within the fortress wall, which they seemed to have since the gates wouldn't have opened yet for the day. That fact would make them seem less suspicious to Kaytan and the guard.

"Who's with her?" Kaytan asked.

The guard shook his head.

"He's the man asking me to care for her," Lerato said. He avoided the word 'Desalian.' With Kaytan here, that would have gotten Miken arrested without a moment's hesitation.

Kaytan nodded slowly. For him, the scene would be little more than a chance to put faces to the stories Lerato had already shared.

"They'll do well in the Citizen's Tournament coming up," Kaytan said as he turned and walked toward the collection of sparing poles.

Either Kaytan didn't notice the heat in the sparing match or he didn't see a reason to worry about it. Lerato tried to turn away as well. Yet as he followed Kaytan the clapping of wood echoed through the air. For the past year Lerato had been gently prodding Alexria for information, but it was hard to do so while also trying not to upset her. His effort to be respectful was battering heads with his curiosity and concern.

A slap sung through the air, the slap of an open hand against skin. It was sharp enough to make Lerato's head turn back toward Miken and Alexria and it was followed by still silence. Alexria was the one with the open hand and Miken's face was turned. Their chests were heaving. Lerato expected a Desalian to retaliate, but Miken did nothing. His two-handed grip on his sparing pole loosened to just one as he looked back to Alexria. His movements were slow now. His face was surprisingly calm. It was Alexria whose eyes were wide, stunned by her own slap. Her open hand was now fidgeting. They stood like that for what felt like a long moment. Then she left. She left her sparing pole standing upright and headed for one of the other entrances. Miken caught her pole as it fell.

Kaytan hadn't noticed the event, since a hit within a training arena was common. Kaytan selected a pole from the rack and tested its weight in his hands.

"I'll join you soon," Lerato said. The words felt abrupt and he started across the arena before Kaytan could question it.

Lerato didn't know what he wanted to accomplish. How was he supposed to begin a conversation with a Desalian he barely knew? Perhaps the relatively calm nature that Miken had about him made him easier to approach. Yet the closer he came, the more tense Miken seemed to be. After Alexria left, Miken paced across their training circle several times. As Lerato neared him, Miken had finally decided to lay down Alexria's sparing pole and continue training with his own. Lerato straightened his shoulders. He had the authority of being Hydia's Prince. He wouldn't let a Desalian intimidate him.

"Where did she go?" Lerato asked. He tried to sound curious instead of demanding.

Miken turned his head as though he only noticed him now. He tapped one end of his pole on the ground. "One of the gardens. She'll come back when she's ready."

"You're not going after her?"

Miken's eyes came up sharp. "She'll come back when she's ready."

That was it? He didn't plan to go after her or talk with her or ask her what she needed?

"She won't recover if all you ever do is wait," Lerato said.

Miken scoffed. "Of course, a prince would know best from his palace life." Sarcasm laced his voice.

"Miken-"

"Why is our business any of yours?"

Lerato knew this was something he should walk away from, that he wouldn't gain anything from staying. The two strides between them began to feel short. Yet before he could turn he had already said, "You made it mine." He at least tried to keep the strength of his voice controlled.

"When?"

"When you made her my responsibility five times in the past year," Lerato said.

Miken's mouth had tightened. A red splotch from the slap was surfacing on his cheek. "You know *nothing*."

"I know what I see. I know I haven't seen her smile in an entire year. And I haven't seen you do anything about it."

Miken's fist swung. Lerato stumbled back as the blow struck his chin.

"No. You know *nothing*," Miken said. "We lost *three* children in *two* days. Three. You can't know what that's like. You can't know."

By the time Miken had finished, the guard was seizing his arms and Kaytan was pushing his way between Miken and Lerato. Lerato rubbed his chin with his thumb. It was throbbing, but manageable. Lerato waved a hand for the guard to loosen his hold on Miken. Lerato stepped past Kaytan to face Miken again. Miken had his chin tipped down and fiery eyes glaring up. He stood waiting for Lerato to strike him back the way any Desalian would have. Yet Lerato couldn't. Three children. The information may have cost him a bruised chin, yet the pain somehow seemed fair in exchange.

Lerato kept his voice low when he spoke, so as not to sound like a challenge. "You're right. I don't know," he said, "but Alex does."

Lerato turned to leave and Kaytan followed close.

"Barely past sunrise," Kaytan said, "and you've already had a threat."

Lerato glanced back and rubbed his chin again. Miken was being escorted out of the arena. "I don't think that was a threat."

* * * * *

When Alexria left the training arena she was struggling to catch her breath. The sparing match itself had left her panting, but after she hit Miken... She hit him. How could she bring herself to do that? She'd never done that. She'd never had the urge or temptation to do that. So why did she? How could she? Alexria could feel her emotions trying to choke her and she walked faster. Her arms were tired. She didn't know how long they had been sparing for. She climbed the first staircase she came to and turned a series of corners that brought her to a long hallway. Her pace quickened to a jog and then to a run. She needed to run. She needed her legs to burn and her chest to heave until she could feel nothing. She needed to feel nothing. She wanted to feel nothing. The hallway blurred past her; the doors, the cobblestone. Her braid thumped against her back. She slowed at the end, turned, and then kept going. She met stairs and she climbed them despite the complaint made by her legs. She climbed the first flight, then the second. Her legs were shaking as she reached the top. She clung to the stone railing to keep her on her feet. She closed her eyes as she tried to breath. In and out. In... and out.

A breeze brushed past her face. She opened her eyes. Sunlight streamed into the torch-lit hall. A balcony, maybe. Legs aching, she walked toward it. The balcony was more than that. She walked out among flowerbeds, small trees, and other greenery of a wide garden. The ocean was in the view on her right, high rolling hills were on her left, and the rocky coast stretched out in front of her. The stars that had been out when they had woken this morning had all hidden by now. Alexria walked between rows of sprouting flowers, budding seedlings, and soft-needled bushes. She reached the far end, marked by a waist-high wall, and looked over the edge at the lower levels of the fortress and the waking Capital city. She must have been on the third or fourth floor of the fortress tower, almost too high for her to sit on the wall ledge. She leaned her hands on it instead.

Home was over those hills. In the past year they had only been there once and that was to put Nevik in charge of the household, the planting seasons, hiring workers, and selling a portion of the harvest. That felt longer than a year ago. Miken had been working with a blacksmith for most of that time. Alexria had only just begun working in the fortress stables. It was familiar to her. She had done that kind of work before she knew Miken and she had sometimes done the odd stable task for her own household. Alexria pulled out the string holding the bottom of her braid. The wind combed through it. The work was good for her. She kept telling herself that.

"Excuse me, miss." A Hydian Guard had come to the garden's entrance. "These gardens are not open to civilians," he said. "I'll need to ask you to leave."

She must have passed by the Guard without noticing. She didn't remember passing anyone. Alexria nodded and started for the door.

"She has brought no harm."

The soft voice drifted to her ears. She had heard it before, but couldn't put a name to it until the Guard stepped aside and the woman took his place.

"I will see to her," the High Lady said. "Thank-you."

The Guard nodded and left. The High Lady Samila, the woman spoken of in legends and stories who had advised Hydian royalty for generations, now walked toward her.

"Good morning, Alexria."

Alexria was at a loss of words. Lady Samila had even knew her name. Lady Samila's gown was as soft as her voice and her long, white hair floated down her back. Alexria was in no way presentable. Sweat laced her shirt and her hair and her braid was still unravelling. Yet Lady Samila's smile didn't seem to notice.

"May I join you on the balcony?" Lady Samila asked.

"Of course, my lady." Alexria stepped to the side to make room, though, after she did, she realized there was plenty of room.

Lady Samila sat softly on the edge of the wall. For generations she has been the High Lady, but her face was as timeless as a young woman's. Alexria had forgotten how timeless Lady Samila's presence felt. It seemed out of place to be standing next to such a woman. But she was also the type of woman who tended to reach out to even the most common citizen.

"It has been a long time since we last spoke," Lady Samila said.

"You remember that?" Alexria asked. They had only met a few times and that had all been five years ago, before she and Miken had left the Capital and settled down in their home.

Lady Samila's smile widened in a soft way. "I forget neither a face nor their story," she said. "I remember your story, Alexria. Though I can see you have grown much in that time."

Alexria glanced down to the pattern of stones on the wall but forced herself to look back up again out of respect. "A lot has happened in that time."

"As life tends to do."

Alexria shook her head. "A lot."

Lady Samila's eyes were deep and warm. "It has weathered you."

"Forgive me, my lady," Alexria said, suddenly realizing who she was speaking to. "I don't mean to trouble you with anything."

The High Lady was bound to have more important matters to deal with.

"Speak, child," Lady Samila said softly. "Tell me what troubles you."

Alexria could feel her emotions swelling up in her throat again. She'd never told anyone about what happened. Miken knew. The servants in their household knew. But actually saying it, actually piecing the memory together into words. That was more than she could do. Her lip trembled. She shook her head and turned to leave.

"Alexria."

The soft voice stopped her but it wasn't enough to turn her. Two gentle hands clasped one of her own as Lady Samila came to stand next to her.

"Oh, child," Lady Samila said. "If I could take this burden as my own, I would. If I could return to the moment that scarred you and rewrite the events, I would. I can see how it has broken you."

Alexria closed her eyes. Her breaths were getting heavier. The tears were coming. How could she let tears come in front of the High Lady? It was the support of her clasp that kept Alexria from running. It wasn't strong enough to pin her there. It wasn't strong at all. It was comforting.

"Alexria, you can become a great woman," Lady Samila said. "I remember seeing that potential in you. I remember seeing that spirit. Child, that spirit may have faded but it is not gone. It is not gone."

Alexria shook her head. A tear slipped out. "I can't. Not now. After everything that's happened..." She waved her free hand as if it would produce the missing words, but nothing more came. She felt a light touch on her chin.

"Look at me, Alexria," Lady Samila said gently.

She did. Lady Samila's eyes glistened as though they were watered by the beginnings of tears.

"Your life is not about what happens to you," Lady Samila said. "It is what you do with the circumstances you are given."

She said it as though it were possible, as though that spirit Lady Samila had seen had a chance of coming back. As though she could be someone and do something, the nightmares would fade away and the memories would stop haunting her. As though she'd be able to breathe again.

"So where do I go from here?" Alexria asked.

Lady Samila's soft smile surfaced again. "Serve others," she said, "the way you had planned to serve your own children."

She said it as though she knew. That was the life Alexria had planned. The simple but fulfilling life of being a mother.

Lady Samila gave Alexria's hand a light squeeze. "To serve may be considered among the lowest of professions, but it is among the greatest acts to offer."

Chapter 7

Coastal Terrain

After the shipwreck

Lerato rested in his cabin until the supplies needed to leave the ship were gathered. He changed his shirt into one that hadn't been ripped by an Etimire. When he was told his wounds were shallow and would be difficult to bandage, he chose to leave them as they were. He was growing accustomed to the ache.

As he jogged up the stairs to the upper deck Alexria fastened a rope to the ship's railing, tugged on it to test the knot, then tossed the remaining coil over the stern. Genev watched nearby bundled in her cloak, holding the bottom of her hood tight beneath her chin. The rain had stopped, finally, yet the wind still had a bite to it.

"The drop would be far less if we began from the lower deck," Genev said.

"It's not as high as it seems," Lerato said.

He turned to look back at the sailors and Hydian Knights on the lower deck. Every man was armed with a sword at his side, a quiver on his back, and a bow in his hand. Some of the Knights were instructing sailors on archery technique. Everyone else looked out into the darkness beyond the ship. Lerato rested a hand on his own sword.

"Lerato," Alexria said.

"Hm?" He skimmed his eyes over the men watching for movement.

"Should I go first?" Alexria asked.

Desalians were bound to be sighted sooner rather than later. They'd need every available arrow and then, once the attack overwhelmed them, they'd need every available sword.

"I'll go last," Lerato said.

He heard Alexria climb over the railing and start down. Lerato shifted his shoulders to test his wounded back. He could still be useful in a battle.

"How well do you know her?" Genev asked.

The question was abrupt enough to gain Lerato's attention. "I've known her a long time."

"An acquaintance and a friendship have two different meanings," Genev said. "We don't know the kind of trouble she'll bring us."

"It can't be much worse than the trouble we've already had."

He started to turn to watch the lower deck again, until Genev gripped his arm. There was strength in her grip as though she were desperate to convince him. Fear was in her pleading eyes.

"She had knowledge enough about the cat to name it an Etimire," Genev said. "Unless we know more of her past, how can we trust her with our future?"

"Genev, I know as much as I need to."

"One of our Knights has even showed concern with her."

This was perhaps her most convincing argument. It was at least her most interesting one.

"Which Knight?" Lerato asked.

"He called himself Adicara," she said. "He said you knew him."

Lerato didn't, yet now wasn't the time to send more fear into her. "For the moment, you need to get off this ship. We'll discuss this later."

* * * * *

The wet rope was slick, even with the grip of Alexria's gloves. It had been a while since she had climbed down a rope, but it wasn't her first time. Miken had made sure she'd learned. She twisted the rope around both her hands. She made a point not to look down where the darkness would make the drop seem intimidating. Instead Alexria focused her eyes on the wood of the ship. She could feel it more clearly than she could see it. The storm had made the boards as slick as the rope. She planted her feet firmly against it and leaned back on the rope's support. Then, one steady step at a time, one sure slide of her hands at a time, she walked down the stern. Her feet only slipped twice. The first was more of a shock to her than anything. Her footing slipped, causing her grip of the rope to slip as well. When her grip tightened, the rope swung the weight of her body hard against the ship. Getting her footing back was harder than she thought it'd be, needing to pull her knees up near her chest before she could manage it. It was similar the second time, but by then she was close enough to the bottom that, after recovering herself, she loosened her grip and slid the rest of the way down. The rocks were jagged and it took a moment to find a solid place for her to stand.

Alexria looked up to where she had come from. She could see two dark figures at the top, one helping the other climb over the railing and hold the rope. Princess Genev crept over the edge, gripping the rope with one hand and the railing with the other. She didn't walk her feet down the stern as Alexria would have done. Instead the Princess was walking, or likely sliding, her hands down the rope and hugging the rope with her knees.

The first time Alexria had used a rope to climb down from a height had been years ago. She had been with Miken and had barely knew him at the time. He had held the rope with one gloved hand and had looped the opposite arm around her. When they had gone over the edge of the railing, they didn't walk or take their time down. They fell. The rope had hissed through Miken's hand and the air had rushed.

Alexria could remember feeling as though her stomach had been pulled up into her throat. She had clung to Miken, trusting him.

Shouts came from somewhere on board the Hydian ship. The Princess froze in place, swaying a little on the rope. She was almost close enough for Alexria to touch her feet if she reached. Lerato disappeared from her view at the railing.

"Keep coming down, my lady," Alexria said. "You're almost there."

There were more shouts. Directions, orders, and battle cries. Some came from the coastal rocks between the ship and the island. Princess Genev began moving again. Instead of watching her come, Alexria found herself looking up at the ship's railing instead. What was she supposed to do if Lerato didn't come. Was the Princess to become her responsibility? Had Lerato planned to let them go ahead? Alexria wished he could trust her enough to tell her that much. She thought he did. She had also thought this trip would be a safe one.

Princess Genev stretched her toes out for something solid. Alexria gently directed her foot to the closest peak of rock within reach. Princess Genev stumbled as she gained a sure footing. She hugged the rope to help steady herself and Alexria caught her by the elbows. Alexria then offered a hand to help her step out of the way for Lerato to climb down, but the Princess ignored it and looked up at the ship instead.

"I haven't seen your brother since you started down," Alexria said.

The Princess stared up the way a child looks intently out the window. "You call him by his name as though he trusts you," she said as she waited for a glimpse of Lerato.

The words surprised Alexria. Lerato had to ask her several times before she began using his name. Even then it had felt awkward and out of place. "I didn't mean to offend you, my lady."

The Princess gave a soft laugh. "And though I'm his sister, I remain a 'lady' to you."

It wasn't age that intimidated her. Princess Genev was about the same age as Alexria, maybe even a little younger. But with her high head and strong voice - and title - Alexria would have taken a retreating step back if the terrain had been easier.

"What would you like me to call you?" Alexria asked carefully.

"I would like you not to be here." The polite words had an edge to them.

The rope whipped back and forth as Lerato appeared at the ship's railing.

"I can protect you if I need to," Alexria said, hoping it wouldn't make things worse.

"Will you?" Princess Genev's gaze was steady when she turned it to Alexria. "Despite what I've heard of you, you still remain the woman who wove her way into the Prince's trust. That will only bring you so far." She looked back up as though she had explained herself.

Despite the many times Alexria had been left in Lerato's care over the years, very little time had been spent with the Princess. Alexria didn't know how to respond to her words. She didn't want to counter her. That was bound to worsen the situation. She wanted to reassure her, but words felt useless to do that. Maybe joining Lerato and Princess Genev as they left the ship had been a poor choice.

Lerato climbed down quickly, rushed almost. His breaths were heavy when he reached them. "We need to go," he said, then began leading the way.

Princess Genev followed, saying nothing about the conversation she'd just had. Alexria also followed quietly, staying at the back of the line.

The travelling was slow. Lerato led them along the rocks closest to the water's edge, where the footing was more dark and wet. Each time Alexria reached to the shadow of a crevice or a ledge she hoped she wouldn't meet some unpleasant surprise. Yet as the battle sounds came closer, she became less concerned about seaweed and more aware of the Desalian men. At first it was only the shouts of commanders and scouts. Then the hiss of arrows became familiar.

Some snapped against the coastal rocks. Each time the wind lifted up, Alexria felt like holding her breath so she could listen closer.

Lerato stopped suddenly and waved for them to crouch down. Alexria felt as though she were hugging the jagged stone that towered up next to her. Then, instead of the nearby snapping of arrows, she heard the pattering of rain. Yet the only water she felt was the mist that showered them with the odd crash of waves against the rocks. The pattering was steady and became louder. Closer. And as it did she recognized it, not as rain, but as shuffling feet. Desalian men scrambling over the coastal rocks toward the Hydian ship.

Alexria forced her breaths to stay calm. She couldn't see the shadows of the approaching men. None of them were this close to the water. Yet the steps were quickly coming closer. Soon she could hear breaths and grunts and whispers. Alexria moved her hand to the dagger on her boot. If she stood up on her toes she would have been able to see above the rocks where the men travelled, but she didn't dare to risk it. She imagined the view would look like the ocean in front of her, yet instead of the water shifting it was the shadows of a sea of men rippling over the coast.

She heard the slide of metal as Lerato drew his sword. It glistened off the light from something. He glanced to her and she shook her head. There were three of them. Two, considering that Princess Genev couldn't fight. They wouldn't accomplish anything now. Maybe if it was ten men, or even twenty. But there would be well over a hundred Desalians shuffling past them in addition to however many were attacking the Hydian ship.

Light flared up at the sound of shattering clay. It was followed by a second and a third, each one flashing up more orange light. Alexria leaned out away from the rock enough to see what had happened. Flames raged across the deck of the Hydian ship and licked up the mast. Something black was thrown and, as it shattered against the stern, the flames spread over the wood. It must have been jars of oil.

"They'll get off the ship, won't they?" Princess Genev said in a whisper. "They wouldn't stay on board?" She'd be thinking of the General, her husband.

The sound of footsteps had mostly faded now. Any nearby Desalians had likely passed by. The firelight glowed on Princess Genev's face as she also leaned out to see the ship, making her worry look more defined. Lerato was in the shadows. The grip on his sword was restless. Alexria manoeuvred over the rocks, around the Princess, until she stood next to Lerato. Any words of comfort she could give would be accepted more by him than by her. His eyes seemed to be flaming as much as the ship. He knew the men onboard better than she did. He was more responsible for them than she was.

"I'm a coward," Lerato whispered.

Alexria took a long breath. She was sure General Kaytan had either dragged him off the ship or close to it. That wasn't something Alexria would be able to do with him, but she needed to at least keep him from going back. "This was a victory for Hydia." She also kept her voice quiet. "They did this to capture the Hydian Royalty. That's the only explanation that makes sense. But we didn't let them do that."

Lerato's face remained hard. It was a look she'd seen on Miken when he had enough frustration to bite back.

"Lerato, you don't always need to be the strong one," she said.

"Says who?"

"You did. A long time ago."

This turned his gaze to her and away from where the firelight danced on the shoreline.

Alexria went on. "We'll get your men back. We can find some way to do that. But for now I need you to keep leading us away from here."

Another large wave rolled up and sent heavy mist showering on them again. She could taste the salt. Princess Genev sheltered her face with her hood. Lerato didn't flinch. He slowly sheathed his sword again, wiped the mist from his face, and then continued leading them away from the Hydian ship.

Chapter 8

With a Limp

14 years before the shipwreck

It was said it had been the strongest winds of this generation, maybe longer. While the Hydian fortress had been relatively unharmed, the Capital itself had enough damage to keep every available hand busy. It would be at least half a month before any help could be sent out to the other small Hydian villages. So Miken and Alexria went themselves. They began with the village furthest from the Capital. It was a small, farming village where all the nearby families came to buy what they needed and sell what they could. Every building had some form of damage done to it. For some, it was a piece of roof or the door that had been torn away by the wind. For others, something heavy had been blown against the side of the building, piercing it, denting it, or tearing some of it away. The street itself was a mess of branches and debris. In the middle of the main street was a neatly built stone well, the closest source of water for these people. Yet the wooden beam across the top had been knocked over in the storm and there was no sign of any roped bucket reaching down to the water.

Miken thought this would have been the first piece of damage to be fixed. Instead all the people of the village were focused on their own tasks, repairing their own buildings and cleaning the street in front of their own homes. So Miken and Alexria began with the well.

Miken tossed a rock into the black hole and he reached four counts before he heard it drop into the water below. They didn't have a rope long enough. As Miken turned and circled, hoping to spot supplies they could borrow, Alexria pointed out something in the hole. It seemed that as the well's rope had fallen during the storm, it had gotten caught on a tangle of roots. Miken could see it dangling near the edge of where the well's walls darkened from dim to black. Miken guessed the distance to be about three counts to it. Though it was out of arm's reach, it was close enough to seem possible to get.

"I'll climb down," Miken said.

Alexria turned her head sharply to look at him. "When was the last time you or I climbed anything?"

Miken was already shrugging off his cloak. "A hole should be easier than a mountain." Judging by the width of the well, he should be able to sit with his back against one wall and his feet against the other. Either that or he could walk down with his hands and feet stretched across the width. It looked simple enough.

"Mike-"

"They need water."

"Then we'll get them water."

He almost thought she wasn't thinking rationally, but he couldn't argue that he was either. "I'll be back," he said.

In the time it took Miken to sit on the stone edge and dangle his legs into the well, Alexria had fetched a rope from one of their saddle bags. It was too short to reach the bottom of the well, but it would be long enough for the distance Miken planned to climb. Alexria tied one end to her horse and tossed the other into the well ahead of Miken. Miken tested how the horse would support his weight before he put his full trust in the rope. The horse grunted and, with Alexria's guidance, could hold Miken's weight over the drop into darkness.

Miken started down with his back and feet on the walls of the well and with a hand on the rope. His breaths echoed in the hole. He didn't realize he was breathing that heavily. Each time he moved down he would send a drizzle of dirt down ahead of him. He worked his way down without looking down for the rope. The first time he did look down, out of curiosity for how much further he had to travel, the depth of the well stared back at him like a black eye. It made his stomach churn in a way he wasn't used to. It made him doubt why he chose to climb down here to begin with. It made his footing slip and he dropped. His back slid against dirt and rocks. He pressed his feet and back harder into the well walls and gripped the rope. He slid to a stop. Debris clouded around him. A moment later he heard debris rain into the water at the bottom.

He sat there for a long moment trying to will his trembling legs to settle. Alexria called down to him and he called back that he was alright. He had to convince himself of that. Miken held the rope tight and looked down again. The rope for the well's bucket was an arm's reach beneath him, tangled in the thick root of a tree. He was almost finished. Miken twisted his hand around the rope supporting his weight and gripped it. Then with his other hand he reached down toward his goal. He could nearly brush it with his fingers. He stretched further, tipping his shoulder down. He slipped again. This time losing his footing on the wall. He gasped as his feet dropped beneath him and then, as quickly as he'd slipped, he jerked to a stop. His hand tightened with pain but that was what had saved him. That single taut rope was what kept him from dropping into the darkness beneath him. Alexria would be up there holding the rope and steadying the horse. And the other rope, the one he had climbed down for, was now dangling in front of him. Miken untangled it out of the roots and, as he was deciding how to hold one rope while climbing the other, he found himself being pulled up. It wasn't very fast, but the circle of daylight above him crept closer. Alexria peered over the edge of the well and it was her arms that helped him climb over the wall to safety. But on the rope, helping the horse pull him up, were five men and a boy from the village. They were all strong, like men who made a living working with their hands.

"They came on their own," Alexria said.

Before leaving the well, Miken pulled up the rope he'd retrieved and tied it to one of the well's thick posts.

One of the five men approached him and stood about a head taller than Miken. "Thank-you," the man said. "From all of us." He looked to both Miken and Alexria when he said it.

"Of course," Miken said. He could feel sweat dripping down his brow.

"I hope you haven't travelled far," the man said.

"We came to lend a hand," Miken said with a shrug. "We thought you could use it." He felt odd saying it. The thought had sounded good. It was something to do. So when the man nodded slowly, Miken wanted to reword what he had said.

This time it was Alexria that spoke up. "Which home is yours?" she asked.

"The blacksmith's shop there," the man said with a motion behind him. The front of the shop was littered with wood and debris and there was a large hole in the side wall of the house behind the shop.

"We can have that wall fixed fairly quick," Miken said. He then looked at the other men that had also helped. "Then we can come help each of you after that."

This time the man's slow nod had an approving smile in it. While Miken helped the man hammer wood over the hole in the house, Alexria cleaned the shop with the family of two boys and their mother. By the time Miken finished, Alexria had convinced the family that others were in need of more help. The boys were eager to go out in the village to do what they could. So that was what happened. The blacksmith and his family divided themselves up and dispersed to help their neighbours and friends. Miken and Alexria dispersed with them.

From there, as each home finished repairing the essentials, the family went out to help others. Soon, people were travelling through-out the village in flocks. Some groups focused on repairing roofs, others repaired walls, and others fences.

Yet it wasn't the overall progress that caught Miken's eye, it was Alexria. For most of the day he worked on a different house than she did. At first he kept track of where she was to ensure her safety. He'd glance in her direction whenever he had a chance to. He never met her gaze so he didn't know if she looked at him as much as he looked at her. Then he saw something that made him pause his work longer than merely a glance. Alexria smiled. It wasn't a forced smile that looked as if her face was straining to keep it. It lit up her eyes enough for him to see from across the street. He hadn't seen why she'd smiled. In a way, that didn't matter to him then. He'd forgotten how much warmth could come from one of her smiles. It brought a feeling into his chest that he hadn't felt in a long time. It made him want to smile himself, and he was sure the corner of his mouth twitched upward without him meaning to. After that each time he glanced toward her it was in hopes of seeing that smile again. He did a few times before the end of the evening. Each time made him feel more warm than the time before that.

When they stopped for the evening, Miken and Alexria were offered a room at the inn for them to stay the night. It was a simple room compared to what they had in the fortress or even compared to the inns in the Capital, but it was shelter for the night. They both sat on the edge of the bed to take off their boots. Miken hadn't realized how much his feet ached until he could stretch and flex them.

"The closest village isn't far," Miken said. "We can go there in the morning if you'd like to do this again."

"I would."

Alexria lightly tossed her boots next to the wall. She sighed and leaned her hands back behind her on the bed. She looked content. He couldn't remember when he last saw her that way.

"You did well today," he said.

The beginnings of a smile flickered over her face. "Thank-you."

Miken brushed his fingers from her chin to her cheek. He didn't realize what he was doing until he was already doing it. He'd forgotten how soft her cheek was and how warm her skin could feel from a day of work. The delicate touch seemed to spread up his arm to his shoulder and into his chest. She closed her eyes. She had such gentle eyes. Her nose was slender. Her mouth... Miken traced his thumb along her bottom lip as he noticed it trembling. He'd forgotten the feeling of it. He'd forgotten the feeling of her.

A tear slipped from her eye. "A year is a long time."

Miken slid closer. She had the faint smell of sweat from a good day's work. He could feel each of her short trembling breaths. He waited for her to move toward him. If her stomach fluttered as much as his, that would be enough to freeze her. Yet as much as he wanted to close the distance himself, he didn't know if he could. It had been so long. Miken moved to her cheek instead and kissed it. He missed the soft touch of his lips on her skin. She had such soft skin. He felt her tension relax. As he pulled away her gaze was down.

"We should sleep," he said softly. "We'll have a long day tomorrow."

Alexria nodded. Miken gave her space to breathe again.

* * * * *

Lerato stacked the three books he had collected. Over dinner the conversation had turned toward Alexria and her presence in the fortress again. Her name wasn't known by the royal family. However they had caught the news that she was put under Lerato's care every now and again. Lerato avoided explaining the fact that Miken was currently in Desalian territory. During the conversation, however, Kaytan had made an interesting comment, saying, "Protecting her is something the Guardians of Hydia would have done."

"They did more important things than that," Lerato's father said as he took another bite of bread.

Kaytan made a light shrug. "That's what they did for me," he said. "I was barely old enough to remember, but I still remember it."

Lerato had found it surprising that Kaytan could remember meeting the Guardians of Hydia and Lerato couldn't. He didn't consider himself that much younger than Kaytan. That was what brought Lerato here, to the library with his sister.

Genev selected the book in the middle which outlined the reign of their grandfather as King of Hydia.

"I thought the Guardians of Hydia lived earlier than that," Lerato said, "and the attack on the Capital had been during their peak years."

Genev flipped through the pages near the end. "The last Guardians of Hydia were killed nearly a few years after I was born. They weren't given their title until... here." She stopped at a page. "For one month this Capital was taken under Desalian control. There were six Hydians in particular that coordinated the attacks to drive the Desalians back out. These Hydians, five men and one woman, were later named the Guardians of Hydia." Genev spent more time in the libraries than Lerato spent in the sparing arenas. She was often his first choice to come to with questions.

Lerato took the chair next to his sister. "But aside from that what-"

The sound of someone knocking at the door drew their attention away from the books. A Hydian Guard stood at the library entrance with Miken next to him. Miken was leaning a hand on the entrance frame and had a saddle bag slung across one shoulder. His right eye was swollen and half-closed.

"What happened to you?" Lerato asked.

While he expected Miken to come in, he stayed where he was instead. "Could we talk?"
He said it as a question instead of a demand.

Miken was supposed to be on the Desali islands for another two days. Alexria was somewhere in the fortress under the protection of another Hydian Guard, as she always was while Miken was away.

"Who is this?" Genev asked.

Lerato stood with a sigh. "A friend," he said, using the title as a way to keep her from worrying. "I'll come back to see what you find." Genev wouldn't need his help anyway.

Lerato motioned for the Guard to be dismissed. Miken didn't start walking until Lerato reached him and, even then, he stayed a step behind him. Lerato led him to an empty dining room not far from the library he had been in. He leaned back on the wooden table to face Miken, who hadn't come far in. The corner of Miken's lip was cut and Lerato was sure there were more injuries hidden under his travelling cloak.

"So, who was the Hydian that did this to you?"

Miken didn't answer right away. Lerato wondered how much of a beating it would take to break Miken's pride. Whatever had happened didn't seem to be enough. That is unless his hesitation was a matter of trust instead.

"This happened in Desali."

Lerato's eyebrows creased. "Your own men did that? Why?"

"It's complicated."

"I'm curious."

It was strange seeing Miken with only one strong eye. It weakened him in a way Lerato hadn't seen before. Miken's one arm was resting on the saddle bag at his side, as though the bag was supporting it. Lerato also got a glimpse of red on Miken's hip, but that was difficult to see beneath his travelling cloak.

"How bad is it?" Lerato asked.

"It's manageable."

"I'm sure it is," Lerato said, letting his disbelief come through in his voice. "Is Alex in any danger?"

"No."

"Could you protect her if you needed to?"

Lerato may not have known Miken very well, but he knew Miken wanted to answer 'yes.' It was his nature to answer 'yes' and to hide all hints of weakness. He was, of course, Desalian. Yet he took too long to answer. There was a point where Miken also seemed to notice this and glanced down and began walking forward. He had a subtle limp and his one shoulder slumped down. Lerato was sure there was more pain than Miken revealed.

"That's why I don't want you sending for her," Miken said.

"Why not?"

"Alex can't know about this."

Lerato scoffed and shook his head. "Do you know what you look like? She's going to find out. There's no way to avoid that. I don't care how good of an actor you think you are."

"I'm here for your help not your advice." Miken had to look away as he spoke those words. How often had he brought himself to ask for help?

If it had been a year ago, Lerato would have assumed this to be a trap set up by the Desalians. The thought grazed through his mind once but nothing more than that. He knew too much about Miken and Alexria now. He'd seen enough of Miken's strong front to notice that he had put that aside this time.

Lerato nodded. "Take a seat, I'll get some water." He started toward the jar and basin at the side of the room. The water would be for Miken's hip and whatever other surface wounds he had. His shoulder would be a separate task that Lerato didn't know what to expect from yet.

"That's not what I need your help for."

Lerato stopped midstride and looked back at him.

Miken reached the table but didn't turn to face Lerato. There was hesitation in him. "Alex doesn't know I'm back in the Capital. And she's not expecting me for another two days."

"And you want me to hide you from her," Lerato said, filling in what was implied.

There were parts of Miken and Alexria that Lerato couldn't understand. He himself would rather go to the support of his wife than hide from her.

Lerato sighed. "What do I tell Alex?"

Miken eased himself into a chair with a wince. He cradled the arm of the injured shoulder. "Nothing. Then you won't have to try lying."

Lerato shifted. He didn't want an argument. It was something they were both very capable of and, in way, he was glad that Miken was too tired for it. "She deserves to know."

"She deserves a lot of things," Miken said. "But this..." He motioned to himself. His voice was quiet when he spoke again. "I've done enough to break her heart already. I can't do it again. Not if I don't have to."

Lerato didn't have anything to counter that with. He wished he knew what Miken had done or what Miken blamed himself for. The wounds seemed minor compared to whatever burden he carried.

"I'm not asking you because you're a prince," Miken said. "Those titles don't mean much to me."

"I've noticed," Lerato said, then regretted his interruption by how much Miken hesitated to continue.

"Lerato, I'm asking you as my friend," Miken said. "And as a friend to Alex as well."

Friend was a new title. It didn't feel fitting yet, but it also wasn't something he would deny. Miken seemed to be the type who trusted few and befriended even less than that. The fact that Lerato was trusted to protect Alexria said a lot of Miken's view of him.

Lerato nodded. "I'm still helping you clean yourself up. I can't leave you here to try and do that yourself."

He went to close the door. Alexria was in the hallway. She stood waiting and listening. She must have seen him from a distance and followed them here. Lerato didn't flinch at the sight of her, nor did he acknowledge her presence at first. He met her gaze, though. He almost invited her in to tend to Miken herself, but held the words back. Miken wanted two days. Lerato didn't know what difference that would make now that Alexria knew he was here, but maybe the time would help Miken recover enough to hide whatever it was he wanted to hide.

Lerato closed the door and returned to Miken. He would need to speak with Alexria later. For now he went to the jars, poured a basin full of water, and brought it back to the table.

Miken leaned his elbows on his knees and opened his saddle bag. "Just leave the basin and I can handle the rest." He pulled a small leather package out of the saddle bag and held it in his teeth as he reached back in.

"Is that Balus Root?" It was a common medicine used for treating open wounds. It worked well, but the sting of it had a sharp bite.

"M-hm." Miken pulled out a cloth and tossed it and the package on the table. "And you won't be around when I use it."

Lerato leaned against the table again. "Can I see your shoulder first?"

Miken glanced up. "My shoulder's fine." Then he used his good arm to soak the cloth in the bowl of water.

"I've seen a shoulder like that before," Lerato said.

Miken didn't look up.

"I know how to help it."

This slowed Miken down until he stopped. He left the cloth in the bowl and shook the water off his hand. When he shrugged off his cloak, he eased it off his bad shoulder.

Before Kaytan was a Captain, he fell off his horse and knocked his shoulder out of place. His shoulder had sagged the way Miken's did now. Lady Samila had talked Lerato through how to reset it and that had been the only time Kaytan had ever swore at him.

Lerato took a breath before he started. "I need your hand."

Miken nodded to where it rested in his lap. Lerato took it, making Miken wince, and took a firm grip around his wrist.

"Now you need to relax your shoulder."

Miken gave a small laugh but then shifted in his seat in an attempt loosen his arm and shoulder. Lerato couldn't tell if it was relaxed as much as it needed to be. Lerato took another breath.

"You've done this before?" Miken asked.

"I have," Lerato said quickly. "I have."

"Then do it."

Lerato nodded and swallowed. An unsettled feeling was building up in him. It was beginning to make him nauseous. All he had to do was pull on his arm and let his shoulder refit into itself. Lerato could remember hearing Kaytan's shoulder pop and seeing the shape of it pop into place with the sound. Kaytan's face had contorted in pain through the whole thing and he'd groaned like nothing else. That was even with a light medicine Lady Samila had given him to help ease the pain.

"Lerato," Miken said. His face was surprisingly calm. "I've had worse. Just do it."

This time when Lerato nodded he followed through and pulled on Miken's arm. Miken made a quiet groan and leaned his head back against the chair and closed his eyes. Lerato lifted his boot to Miken's side to keep it back as he leaned his weight back with Miken's arm. This made Miken groan again. Miken's stone face winced and twitched. His breaths became sharp. Yet it didn't seem to be working. Lerato was only causing more pain. He wondered if Miken's shoulder was relaxed enough, but his hand seemed to be. It was his other hand that gripped at the armrest as though he wanted to rip it off the chair. Then Miken fainted. His head slumped down, his whole torso released its tension, and the lump of his shoulder popped back into place. Lerato felt the jerk through Miken's arm and it worsened the nauseous feeling in his stomach.

Lerato took a step back to recover from it himself. Again he took a breath. This time long and slow. Miken had fainted. It was something Lerato never would have been able to picture. Yet there was Miken pale, slumped over, and vulnerable in the chair in front of him.

Lerato wrung out the wet cloth in the basin and went to put it on Miken's face to help wake him. He paused when he noticed Miken's back. There were two thin rips on the back of his tunic. The skin beneath his tunic was red. It wasn't the pale red of a slap. Instead it was the bright red lashes from a whip. Lerato carefully peeled back one of the rips as much as he could to glimpse many lashes scattered all across Miken's back. It made sense for Miken to have fainted with both his shoulder resetting and his aching back being pressed into the chair. Lerato touched the cool cloth to one side of Miken's face while he lightly tapped his opposite cheek.

Miken startled awake and grabbed the collar of Lerato's tunic. "Mehera," he said in a breath as he looked about his surroundings. When he noticed Lerato, he released him and asked. "Are you alright?"

"That was my question for you," Lerato said. He readjusted his tunic and put the cloth back on the table.

Miken returned his attention to his own shoulder as though he had just remembered it.

"It should be set," Lerato said.

Miken rubbed his shoulder and slowly shifted it forwards and backwards. Miken's wrists were red, the way restraints could make them to be.

"Mehera..." Lerato started, unsure of where he wanted to go with it. Perhaps being blunt was the easiest option. "Is that the man who had you beaten?"

"Why would you say that?" Miken asked. He was still focused on testing his shoulder.

"I saw your back after you fainted."

Miken eased himself out of his chair and tested how his arm hung on its own. It seemed to be manageable. He spread the wet cloth out on the table, opened the package of Balus Root medicine, and sprinkled the powder over the cloth.

"Did Mehera do this to you?" Lerato asked again.

Miken gave a weak half-smile. "Mehera," he said as he began pulling off his tunic with his good hand, "would gladly do this if he could find the excuse."

"Who is he?"

"My younger brother." Miken managed to remove his tunic and toss it onto the table. He was a strong man. Yet as he turned to adjust the cloth he revealed the unfriendly collection of lashes over his back. Miken climbed up to sit on the table. "I'm lucky, though, for a Desalian," he added. "At least my brother would rather beat me than kill me."

Both the sight and the thought made Lerato's stomach tighten. "A fight is something I could picture for you," Lerato said. "You're someone who's quick to defend himself. But this..."

"It's complicated." Miken lowered himself down so he lay on the table with his back on the cloth. He only winced once and it was subtle. His breaths were deep.

"I feel I should know," Lerato said. He leaned his hands on the edge of the table.

Miken smiled. This time it was an amused one. "This is certainly the most interesting interrogation I've seen." He readjusted his back on the table and looked up at the ceiling. "Have you heard of the plague that swept through Desali?" he asked.

"Vaguely." It had reached the Hydian Capital and some villages, but there weren't enough deaths in Hydia to call it a plague.

"It struck Desali hard enough for the trust among the people to shatter," Miken said. There was tension in his voice, likely from the medicine's sting. "It's reached the point where each island has isolated itself from the others. They're not letting anyone new ashore. Desalian or not."

"But you went ashore anyway," Lerato assumed.

"I had something I needed to find."

"Did you find it?"

Miken was slow to answer. "I ran out of time to look." He motioned to his face. "This was from my arrival." He jerked a thumb back toward his back. "My stay." Then he motioned to his hip and shoulder. "And my departure."

"Would they come after you?" Lerato asked. On any other occasion Miken could likely look after himself.

Miken adjusted his back again. His mouth flinched a little. "They've made their point."

Lerato nodded slowly. It seemed Miken had said all he planned to say. "Well," Lerato said, searching for what he wanted to say, "I suppose I'll leave you to look after yourself."

Lerato started toward the door.

"Thank-you," Miken said finally.

Lerato turned and gave another nod. "Thank-*you*."

As he went into the hall and closed the door behind him, he found Alexria waiting there. She sat with her back against one of the stone pillars and so Lerato sat against the pillar next to her. It was different with her. Though she was physically unharmed, she seemed just as fragile.

"How much did you see?" Lerato asked gently. He kept his voice quiet so it wouldn't carry into the room for Miken to hear.

"Enough," Alexria said just as quietly. She gave a weak shrug. "I know it happened while he was in Desali. And I know he doesn't want me to know."

Lerato didn't know what would happen if he told her more. Would she even want to know?

"He wants two days," he said. "He'll need more than that to recover, but that should be a good start."

"You're not going to let me see him, are you?" She said it as though she had already accepted the fact.

"No, I'm sorry." He may not completely understand Miken's decision, but it was still Miken's decision. Lerato didn't know enough to be able to break his promise.

Alexria nodded and looked down at her hands.

"He'll be safe and well taken care of," Lerato said. "I promise."

She took a long breath. "He's lucky to have a friend he can go to."

Did she wish she was that friend? Did she wish Miken had come to her instead and asked her to tend to him? As much as Lerato tried to search for those answers in her face, he couldn't see them.

"He loves you," Lerato said. If there was one thing he could assure her with, it was this.

A broken smile crept on the corner of her lips. "I know."

Chapter 9

Stars

After the shipwreck

Lerato led Princess Genev and Alexria along the rocky shoreline until the burning ship was at least four arrow shots away. He kept a steady pace. The further the ship was behind him the less likely he was to turn back. The light of morning crept up on them and was mostly hidden in the overcast skies. The black shadows of the island and the ocean quickly became grey and blue. The Desalian island of Petayrn slowly took shape. Each time his steps bobbed him up high enough to see more, Lerato took the chance to look. Most of Petayrn had been divided into farmland. Homes and barns were scattered throughout the view. The area they had reached was a thick forest that covered the rest of what Lerato could see. In the distance, just above the tree tops there was the peak of a mountain. If there was any kind of Desalian stronghold, he guessed it would be near there.

Lerato began to climb up the coastline rocks toward the forest, keeping himself low and looking around him for Desalians.

"The ground will be soft from the storm," Alexria called in a whisper. "We can't leave footprints. Especially here."

Lerato paused, nodded, and then continued on with careful steps. He stepped on rocks as long as he could, however the rocks soon became covered with soil. Occasional rocks were scattered on the dirt and Lerato moved from one to the next. Some thick roots also twisted above the soil and he stepped on these when he needed to. The forest was thick enough to have been growing as long as the island had been here. There was sure to be plenty of places for them to stay hidden. The wind made the forest look alive as it swayed branches back and forth. There were no Desalians that he could see. He hoped the forest would be a rarely traveled place. As Lerato glanced to the side, in the direction of the ship, he noticed a shadow of movement. He paused briefly to look. It was a crowd of the Desalian army that had attacked the Hydian ship. The men were now returning to their own stronghold. The battle would now be over. Lerato only hoped most of the Hydians had survived for them to rescue. Yet how would they rescue them? They were still vastly outnumbered. He and Genev were still royalty that needed to remain hidden. It was pointless to hope of making a successful rescue any time soon.

Lerato reached the shelter of the tree line and looked back. Genev had already started toward him. She set her hands down carefully as her sandaled feet made their way up and across the coastal rocks. She didn't look nearly as fluent as Alexria who followed behind her wearing boots instead. Genev wasn't suited to be out here. Lerato's only consolation was that the alternative option was for her to be taken prisoner by the Desalians.

Alexria glanced to the side and then stopped and crouched down. She must of seen the Desalian army as well. She paused there for a moment to watch them before she continued on.

"I saw them too," Lerato said as Genev and Alexria reached them. "Nothing's changed from before."

"It's a small island," Alexria began.

"That gives us less places to hide." Hide was what they needed to do now.

"A small island will have a small army," Alexria said instead. She motioned to where they had seen the crowd. "If they sent that many men to take the Hydian ship, that would leave very few behind to guard their stronghold."

The thought gave Genev a spooked look. "That's not where we want to go."

"Maybe it is," Lerato said, holding up a hand to settle his sister. The thought was tempting. "You think we can free the crew?"

"I can't," Genev said. "I won't venture any closer to a Desalian. I've heard enough stories of what happens to prisoners."

Lerato recalled what Miken had looked like after some Desalian men had turned on him. His striped back and beaten body was a picture of reality in Desalian prisons.

"That will happen to our men if we don't help them," Lerato said.

"That will happen to us if we do," Genev said. "You can't let her use you like this."

Lerato took her flailing hands in his to help settle her. "Adicara lied to you about her. The man doesn't exist. I don't know the name."

"Adicara was on the ship?" It was Alexria who asked the question and it was her turn to look spooked.

"He was," Lerato said. "How do you know him?"

Alexria's gaze was elsewhere as though she were recalling her time on the ship or some other memory.

"Is he a friend?"

"No." She was quick with this answer.

"Then how do you know of him?"

Alexria shook her head. "We can't go to the fortress. Not with him there."

"How do you know he'll be in the fortress?" Lerato asked.

"He will be." She sounded convinced and certain. "We need to find a place to hide through the day."

"I told you before," Genev said, "we shouldn't be trusting her."

"Genev..." Lerato held up a frustrated finger to silence Genev and then went to Alexria. There was still too many gaps of information and too many questions hanging unanswered. "I need more than that," he said to Alexria.

Alexria looked at him with a subtle grimace. "You've respected our past before," she said quietly. "Don't change that now."

"The situation's different now."

She looked as though his words pained her, yet perhaps that was a good thing now. Perhaps he needed to break her a little to get some truth out of her. He had no more patience otherwise.

When she still didn't answer, he added, "Alex, we're in the Kingdom of Desali. The chances of us getting back to Hydia are very low."

"It's been done before," Alexria said.

"By Guardians of Hydia," Lerato said, with frustration finally snapping into his voice, "not forty Hydians and their royalty. We need every advantage we can get. Even if that means tearing open your past, but I don't know what else to do."

"My past won't help you," Alexria said quietly.

"But something will."

She started to turn but Lerato grabbed her chin. His grip was stronger than he intended and she closed her eyes. Her breaths became heavy.

"You're better than this," Alexria whispered.

She was right. He didn't know where his temper had lashed from, but it wasn't in his nature. Lerato let her go. She stayed stiffened where she was as she settled her breathing.

"This Etimire takes orders from Adicara," Alexria in a fragile voice. "That's all I can tell you. I'm sorry."

* * * * *

They found a tall evergreen nearby, one where the needle-branches draped to the ground around it like a dress. Princess Genev fit in the sheltered space by the trunk. They stored the supplies under the tree as well. Lerato and Alexria each took watch on either side of the tree. Alexria found a large boulder to sit behind, rest against, and peer over. She brought some pieces of bread from their bag of supplies so she wouldn't need to return to the evergreen for food through the day. Returning to the evergreen would also mean returning to the Princess and Alexria wasn't ready to do that anymore than she had to.

The day passed by slow, but quiet. The boulder's shadow circled around her as morning turned to evening. The quiet of the forest felt safe for now, but it also made her anxious. It was a race between a Hydian rescue or Desalian capture. And all they were doing was waiting for the winner. It made for a long day to sit alone.

As evening faded close to night, Alexria had the odd feeling that someone was nearby. She hadn't seen any movement and the trees blocked most of the wind, but she couldn't shake the fear that was growing over her. Her eyes darted through the forest at sounds that weren't even there. Her fear was playing with her.

Then she saw it. Not a man. It was too small and too high in the branches. It moved slow but easily from branch to branch. It flowed through the path of the shadows. A tail swayed in the air and then curled back toward the dark bundle.

She wanted to think that it didn't know they were here, but she knew better than that. She glanced around her, expecting to see Adicara coming from the opposite direction. Aside from Lerato, no one else was in view.

Alexria drew her dagger. The sound of her blade sliding through its sheath must have been louder than she thought. Lerato and the Etimire both seemed to hear it. Lerato drew his own blade and started toward her. The movements of the Etimire seemed less subtle now. It seemed less concerned with remaining in the shadows, hidden, and more directed toward them. Hopefully she and Lerato were all it was aware of, and not Princess Genev. With a pounce, the Etimire vanished from sight.

"What is it?" Lerato whispered as he reached her.

"The Etimire's back."

There was a rustle of leaves above them, then silence, then, in a blur of movement in the corner of her eye, it landed on the boulder Alexria was crouching beside. Alexria jumped up in instinct and held her dagger ready. The Etimire's tail flicked back and forth with a patient rhythm.

"Why isn't it moving?" Lerato asked, his sword also ready.

The Etimire's pale, wide-eyed gaze was steady on Lerato. The eyes didn't graze over him or watch his sword, they were focused on his face. The cat's nose twitched.

Alexria thought for a moment and then spoke a phrase in the Muglaunian Tongue to ask what it wanted. In a blink, the Etimire's gaze moved to her and its tail tossed. Lerato also looked at her, but only in a glance.

When the Etimire spoke it was with a rough, snarl-like voice, but the sounds formed words in the Muglaunian Tongue that Alexria could make out. "*From men you can run. From men you cower in hiding. Yet I succeed always. My prey are found always.*"

"Alex?"

The Etimire's nose twitched again. "*You're blood is not royal,*" it said in the foreign tongue.

"No, I'm not." Alexria said, assuming it could understand at least some Common Tongue.

With a series of blinks it looked at Lerato, looked to the evergreen, then back to Alexria. "*Your company is unfortunate for you.*"

"Alex," Lerato said, stronger this time.

"I think you're its target," Alexria said.

Lerato shifted his stance. "And where's Adicara?"

"*Adicara's regards have been sent,*" the Etimire said as though to answer him.

The mention of his name brought Alexria back to her home in the countryside, to her room, to that night. She had been helpless back then. She had been trapped in Adicara's grip back then. But now was different. Now she could do something. Now she was not only familiar with a blade, she was skilled with one. Alexria traded her drawn dagger for her sword in a single motion.

"He's not here," Alexria translated for Lerato. She wished he was, but his cat was good enough.

Lerato spoke up before she could and he said the very words that Alexria was beginning to form in her mind. "I say we kill it."

The Etimire's eyes narrowed. Its spine flattened and its shoulders pulled back. Its tail hovered low to the boulder's surface. Both Alexria and Lerato held their swords high and ready. Lerato made the first move, swiping his sword toward it. The Etimire leapt toward Alexria's side of the boulder. She made a swing of her own, also missing. The cat darted backwards into the branches. It could be heard dashing through the forest around them in one direction and then the other, but the darkness of dusk hid any sight of it. Alexria found herself circling in an attempt to follow the sound. The Etimire wasn't leaving, it was preparing. Her heart pounded in her chest. She saw the occasional streak of movement.

Then it was suddenly darting toward them. Alexria slashed her sword back and forth near the ground, forcing it in another direction. The Etimire ran away again and then she heard Lerato do the same thing from somewhere behind her. Lerato cried in pain, limped, then straightened back up again. Again the Etimire could be heard circling them in the forest.

"Lerato, stand back to back," Alexria shouted to him.

He did without question or hesitation.

The Etimire darted in and out of the forest. Sometimes low against the ground, sometimes on lower branches near them. Either Alexria's or Lerato's sword was there to meet it. The shadows of the forest played with her eyes. She did her best to watch the movements and follow the sound. It would leap out of the forest so suddenly that her movements felt more like instinct than a choice. Her eyes felt tired and she could feel herself sweating. How could she be fighting hard enough to be sweating already? How long could they keep doing this? Alexria shook her head to focus on the cat again.

The fast, wide sweeps of her sword were working. Their defence seemed flawless until the Etimire stopped on the boulder just outside their reach. Its eyes danced over the evergreen and the ground around it. Its nose twitched. Then it darted back and up and the rustle of branches was in the direction of the evergreen. Toward Princess Genev. The Princess screamed. The Etimire had jumped into the higher branches and would be weaving its way down. Alexria ran to the tree, dropped, and slid across the ground under the lowest hanging needles and into the darkness beneath it. A shower of twigs half-blinded her. She drew the dagger from her boot. The dark cat landed on the branch above her and made a terrible snarl. The outline of a tail drooped within reach and Alexria swung her blade. The Etimire shrieked in pain. The shriek was as sharp as a crack of thunder and the sound likely carried and echoed over the whole island. Alexria covered her ears. By the time the forest had stopped echoing the sound, the Etimire had raced away from them and into the distant shadows. The forest, and the night, was still again.

* * * * *

When the sound of the Etimire faded to silence, Lerato finally let himself sit. His calves throbbed with the pain caused by the Etimire's claws. He was sure there'd be blood, but the dim light of dusk wasn't enough to see how much. He touched the throbbing area with tender fingers. The pain made him wince. There were two cuts across his right calf and three more painful cuts across his left.

Slow movement came from under the tree as Alexria crawled back out into the open.

"Are you both alright?" Lerato asked.

Alexria nodded. "You're not."

Lerato scoffed. He wasn't sure if it was at her comment or because he was, once again, injured. "I'll kill that cat," he said through gritted teeth.

Alexria sat on the ground near him and handed him a cloak. "In a way, I hope you won't have a chance to."

Lerato took the cloak she offered him. "What's this for?"

"To tear up and bandage your wounds," she said.

Lerato wouldn't have thought to use a cloak for a bandage, but it seemed they didn't have many other options. He drew his dagger and tore of a strip of cloth.

"You know more than I thought you did," he said, hoping the conversation would help take his mind away from his wounds. "How did you know the Etimire could speak?"

Alexria made a weak shrug. "I've asked Lady Samila about them before."

Lerato wrapped the first strip of cloth around the middle of his left calf and tied it tight. His wound complained at the pressure. "Where did you learn to speak it?"

She was slower to answer this question. "I learned a long time ago."

It was another piece of her past that she left hanging. It reminded him of the conversation that they had this morning and that Lerato had been recounting through his mind all day.

"I spoke out of place earlier," Lerato said. "It was an improper display of my temper and I apologize."

A half-smile twisted the corner of Alexria's mouth. "You sound like a Prince when you talk like that." Her tone was light.

Lerato laughed quietly at himself as he tore up more cloth. "My father would be proud," he said. Then after a pause, added, "While Miken would say I was trying too hard."

"I think he wishes you weren't royalty."

"Hmm," he said in agreement, then winced as he pulled a bandage too tight. "I don't think he's ever called me 'Sir.' You, I remember I had to ask you several times to call me by my name before you ever did. While Miken..."

"There's more to him than what he lets people see."

A light breeze rippled through the forest, making the branches above them sway. He could see patches of the darkening sky through the leaves. As the branches settled, he could make out the spot of a star.

"Why do you trust him?" Lerato hoped the question came across as subtle. Yet it was something he had wondered for a long time.

Alexria took her time to consider the question. "Why do you trust *me?*" She asked the question gently.

"You're not Desalian." The answer was simple.

"You know as little about my past as you do about his."

Her words quieted him. Until this morning, he had never thought much about her past. However her argument was a valid one. Lerato slowly tied the last of his bandages and then leaned his hands on the ground behind him. "I've heard Lady Samila say that, unlike love, trust is often conditional," he said. "She's also said it's a vulnerable virtue."

"Vulnerable?"

Lerato smiled. "It involves taking a risk," he said.

Alexria offered a weak shrug. "You've risked trusting him before."

Lerato sighed and looked up in search of the stars. The question tormenting him was if he could do it again.

Chapter 10

Skillfully Armed

10 years before the shipwreck

Alexria may not be able to sprint faster than Miken, but she could keep up with him if she had to. That was what they did now. The two of them sprinted down a worn, riverside path and she stayed as close behind Miken as she could bring her legs to. The river was roaring. The water swelled high on the riverbanks and threatened the path they sprinted down. There was no one else on the path, thankfully. It would have slowed them down. A coil of rope bounced in Miken's hand. That was the only thing he grabbed from his horse before the two of them raced off down the path. The rope was to rescue the boy being swept down the river's current. Thankfully the boy managed to keep his head above water and visible most of the time.

Their sprint was just enough to catch up to the river's current, but by the time they were running beside the boy Alexria's legs were burning. The fact that Miken kept sprinting meant that he planned to jump in the water, and they'd need to get ahead of the boy in order to do that.

Alexria pressed onward, swinging her arms hard to keep her legs moving fast. The boy wouldn't have much more time. Just as it seemed that her legs couldn't go any further, Miken called her name and tossed the coil of rope in the air. He had one end of the rope in his hand when he jumped into the brown water. Alexria slowed and caught the coil of rope. It unravelled fast. She looped the rope around a thick tree and held on tight as the coil was stretched out and pulled taut. Miken and the boy had both been forced under water by the current, but Miken would be climbing up the rope's length with the boy somehow wrapped in his arms or clinging to his back. Alexria pulled at the rope to help them, leaning back and even putting a foot against the tree to add more strength to her strain. Their lungs would be straining. Looking through the muddy water they wouldn't have been able to see the surface any more than she could see them. They'd just need to hope it was there. They'd need to keep holding on. Alexria pulled harder on the rope. The water swelled up over something and then two heads slowly emerged from the rushing water. The boy was gasping and coughing. Alexria's hands stung from the rope's bite, yet she held on and pulled with everything she had until Miken and the boy were climbing up the riverbank.

Miken was always the one to take the risks. Whether that meant climbing down into a well or jumping into a river, he was the one to do it. And if he had been taking risks so that she wouldn't have to, then maybe she could accept it. But it was more than that. The longer he had to wait between taking risks, the more restless he became. And he was always quiet after the danger had passed, the same way he was quiet after his trips to Desali. As if he hadn't found whatever satisfaction he was looking for.

After they had crawled out of the river, Miken sat on the riverbank while Alexria returned the boy to his family, who had also run down the path after them. The embraces were warm and the smiles were relieved. When they had all left, Alexria sat next to Miken on the ground. Some strands of his hair dripped beside his eyes as he stared out at the river. The water churned and lashed along its course. Its steady voice drowned out any songs from the forest.

"I still look for Allia," Miken said.

His pained words startled Alexria. They'd come as suddenly as a fish leaping from the river. It left her without anything to say in return.

"I can't stop myself from looking," he said without turning to her. "Each time I go to Desali."

Alexria closed her eyes and rested her head on his shoulder. Miken looped an arm around her hip.

"I know you do," she said.

The half-embrace of his arm was warm and drew her closer to him. He seemed to need her close to him.

* * * * *

Kaytan brought the pile of pages to the table. "Two thieves found near the Northern Forest. A horse thief *and* several of his horses at Kyda's Lake. Three other thieves, each found in the area of the Capital. And a pair, brothers wanted for some time now, were tracked through Cardinal Valley and past the Rylan border until they were caught." With each thief that was mentioned, Kaytan slapped a Wanted poster on the table. "These were all caught this year."

Lerato leaned back in his chair. "That's not very many."

"The same two people brought in them all."

Lerato let his eyebrows raise. "Two." He counted six Wanted posters. That was over half of what a handful of Hydian Knights and Guards could accomplish in the same time. "Who are they?"

"We don't know." Kaytan said it as though he was proposing a puzzle.

"Someone has to know."

"Then that someone is keeping it quiet," Kaytan said. He waved a hand over the posters. "Each of these men were left bound near the Western Gate with their poster pinned to the door with an arrow. The Guards on duty on the wall say the two people delivering them wore hooded cloaks to stay hidden. The prisoners say they were caught by a man and a woman. No names."

Lerato leaned his elbows on the table and tapped a finger on the wood. He's watched the Citizen's Tournament every year. There were plenty of men with enough skill to accomplish something like this. There were even a handful of women that also seemed capable enough. Yet the amount of time needing to be devoted to tracking these thieves seemed more than what most could afford. Most would need time to work and feed their families. Most couldn't survive without earning their living. So what did these two want out of this?

"I haven't shown this to your father," Kaytan said.

This surprised Lerato, being the first time to have heard this, but then he smirked. "So the new General is dodging the King already."

"I'm not that new."

"Three seasons is new."

Kaytan's gaze flickered down and his shoulders shifted.

"I'm honoured you came to me," Lerato started. "I am. -"

"Do you know the stories of the Guardians of Hydia?" Kaytan asked.

"Everyone does," Lerato said with a shrug. "But that was a generation ago."

Kaytan sat in the chair behind him and leaned forward. "What are they chances that they're the ones doing this?"

"They were all killed a long time ago."

"That was never confirmed for all of them." Kaytan seemed convinced of the possibility.

Lerato shook his head. "By now... they'd all be... old. Older than my father."

Kaytan stared back down at the posters.

"It makes more sense for them to be new people," Lerato added. "Though calling them 'Guardians of Hydia' is a strong title."

Kaytan planted a finger on the Wanted poster of the two brothers. "I heard the title from them," he said. "Whether we agree or not, it seems there are already rumours of new Guardians of Hydia."

"And you say it's about time," Lerato said, filling in his General's words.

Kaytan leaned back and folded his arms. "A generation ago there was hope of ending this war with Desali. This kingdom needs that kind of hope again. These two people may be the ones to do that for us."

"Even if they're two stray Hydians without a name?"

"Even if they're two stray Hydians without a name. The same way some of the old Guardians of Hydia started."

It was Lerato's turn to wave a hand over the posters. "Why not tell all this to my father?"

"I mean no offense by it," Kaytan said, "but your father would see this pair as a threat."

"Then I must be my father's son." 'Threat' was almost too strong a word. It wasn't that he didn't appreciate the efforts made by 'this pair.' It was likely their actions were genuine. Yet it was the hooded cloaks and the hiding of names that made Lerato uncomfortable.

"These two people," Kaytan said, "whoever they are, need to be protected more than they need to be revealed."

Guardians of Hydia. There were once six of them. When Desali overtook the Hydian Capital a generation ago, it had been those five men and one woman who led the attack to regain the city. Lerato gave a nod. "Then I'll convince my father to agree."

* * * * *

After Miken had finished binding the thief and Alexria had pinned the Wanted poster to the Western gate, they remounted their horses a short distance away where they could watch the thief in the shelter of the shadows. The Western Gate wouldn't open until dawn, like all the gates in the Hydian fortress, but that time was quickly approaching. Miken and Alexria would wait until the thief was in the hands of Hydian Guards before they went any farther. The routine had become familiar by now.

Miken handed Alexria a skin of water to let her drink first. They'd found the thief yesterday in a rough, forest camp between two villages. Miken had tracked him to there. Miken and Alexria had then watched and followed the man until they saw him threatening some travellers on the road and trying to steal their whole cart of grain. This was when Miken and Alexria stepped in. After they'd chased the thief on horseback, clashed swords, and finally bound him, it was late afternoon. They had to ride hard through the night to reach the Capital by dawn. Luckily this man hadn't put up a struggle along the way. Some men do.

"How long until you go to Desali?" Alexria asked, finishing with the water and handing it back.

"Four days," Miken said. "It may be easier to stay in the Capital than to go anywhere else." Then after a thought he added, "Or I could leave early so I could return early." Four days would be a long time for him to sit still and do nothing.

Alexria nodded but didn't seem to be leaning more toward one option or another.

The night air was cool, making it refreshing to breathe after a long ride. It was a good night to have to wait. Most mornings had not been as fortunate with sharp wind and chilling rain. Yet this was easily durable. Even for the bound up thief.

"When you're in Desali," Alexria said, "is this what you do?" She made a small nod toward the thief.

For ten years Miken had been travelling back and forth between Alexria and the islands. For a handful of those years there had been children to return to as well. She's never asked about what he did. She's never wanted to know.

"I do a lot of things," Miken said.

She was quiet again for a long moment. They were close enough to the edge of the city to hear crickets in the rolling fields.

"Is this how you look for Allia?" she asked.

If Allia were still alive she'd be living in one of the well-built Desali fortresses. Searching for her was very different from searching for rough men living off the land between Hydian villages. But none of that was what Alexria was looking to hear.

Miken circled his horse around so he could face her. The morning light had lifted enough for him to see her face well in the shadows. "Alex, I know I can find her." His plea came through in a whisper. "I just need more time."

"It's been four years." She sounded tired. Part of it may have been from the journey. "You don't even know if she's out there."

"If I stop looking and she *is* there..." But he didn't know how to put the rest of it into words. The weight that burdened his shoulders when he returned home empty handed seemed to tire him more each time. "We can still go back to how things were. We still have that chance. We don't have to keep living like this."

Alexria was shaking her head by this point. The corners of her mouth twitched with emotion. "What if we did? What if this life, right now, is all we ever know."

This life wasn't what he had pictured for the two of them. This life left them sleeping outdoors more often than not. It left them looking over their shoulders and drawing their swords.

"We're helping people," Alexria said. "We are. We're rebuilding homes and making this kingdom safer for families." She gave a weak shrug. Her bottom lip trembled. "We've helped a lot of people... But I don't know how to help *you*."

"It's not your place to." The words came out too fast. Too blunt.

He expected her to look away or to shy away from what she was trying to say, but she kept pressing on as though the words had been sitting in her heart longer than he had been aware.

"What you're looking for," she said, "...that moment in time when we had a family and a home... Mike, we can't get that back."

"Alex-"

"It's gone."

Miken looked away.

"It's gone."

Miken squeezed his eyes closed. The words were soft but they hit him hard. He was stronger than this. Her hand, the soft skin of her hand, slid around his.

"Mike."

Everything about him was tense. It kept himself from shaking. Her thumb stroked the back of his hand.

"Miken."

His eyes opened. Her gaze, through fragile and moist around the edges, was as soft as her touch.

"You need to stop looking," she said, almost too quiet for him to hear.

She brought her other hand to the side of his face. Her cool touch refreshed him.

"You need to stop looking."

* * * * *

After the thief had been taken in by the Hydian Guards, Miken rode down to the shoreline to sit alone on the rocks. The sky was still dim as it waited for the sun and the morning was quiet. Every other time Miken had come here, it had been after he'd returned from a trip to Desali. It felt out of place for him to be here now. The Hydian shoreline was a place for him to clear away everything he'd seen in Desali, as well as everything he'd done. So what did he need to clear out now? He had spent this past season scattered across Hydia to stay busy in whatever ways he could. He never stopped long enough to think. He couldn't afford to think. Yet now that Alexria mentioned Allia's name, all he could picture was the life they used to have in their little corner of Hydia. He was wasting time. Every building they rebuilt, every thief they bound, and every wandered-off-child they found was all time Miken could have spent searching for Allia. It was something Alexria wouldn't understand. Everything they'd done for the people of Hydia had somehow brought life back into Alexria. He couldn't take that away from her.

Miken noticed movement in the corner of his eye. It was a fisherman. Specifically it was the same fisherman Miken had seen walking this shoreline every morning he sat here. He carried the same fishing pole and had filled the same bucket of fish. He also wore the same friendly grin.

"Mornin', sir," the fisherman said in his usual greeting.

Miken offered his usual friendly wave. They never spoke much more than that. The fisherman would pass on by and continue to the docks, leaving Miken to watch the horizon. Yet this time the fisherman sat down. He found a smooth rock next to where Miken was sitting, put down his bucket and settled down onto it. Miken was too surprised at first to say anything.

"A sunrise like this one I'll not want to be missin'," the fisherman said.

The sky was a dim scattering of pale sky and clouds. It wasn't anything impressive. "You sat for a sunrise?"

"Small things, son. Small things," the fisherman said with his grin.

Miken didn't understand but he still looked out at the sky again.

The fisherman pointed with a painter's hand. "See the gap there in the clouds. The sun's eye will lift there. And before that you'll be treated with a dance of colour, you will."

Miken could picture it.

"And come, say, midday, those clouds will rain just enough water to lift the heat from those workin' through the day." The fisherman gave a content sigh and leaned back on his hands.

"How do you know all that?" Miken asked.

The fisherman shrugged. "Many men work beneath the mornin' but you won't find many to stop and look at it," he said. "They catch the fish but miss the smell of the ocean."

Miken found himself taking a deep breath through his nose before he realized it. The air was cold and salty.

"Good, isn't it?" The fisherman took a deep breath himself. "The smell of home."

Miken tried to smile but it felt weak. The fisherman was one of those men that was full of folk wisdom and tales. He'd play along if he had to. "What if you spend so much time smelling the ocean, that you miss the fish you need to survive?"

"Hmm." The fisherman leaned his elbows on his knees in the same way Miken was sitting. "Lost something, did you?"

This man was a stranger. Miken had no reason to trust him with anything considering that Desalian spies were more common than even Miken knew. Yet maybe being a stranger was a good thing. He was a new ear that didn't know enough to judge him and who Miken didn't need to see again.

"I did," Miken said.

The fisherman nodded. "I saw the burden in you," he said gently.

Miken wanted to wince knowing his weakness had been so visible. "So, you just sat for the sunrise?"

The fisherman's smile was soft. "Have you ever seen the sky after a good storm? The kind that shakes trees and sends rivers rushin'."

"You're changing the subject."

This only widened the fisherman's smile. "The sky after a storm is the clearest you'll ever find," he said. "Like the sky's clutter just needed cleanin'. But you can't see the sky 'till you've sailed through the storm."

Maybe the subject hadn't been changed. "You can see the same sky if you stay in the harbour," Miken said in counter.

"True enough," the fisherman said with a nod. "But I'd argue ship's are built to be sailed. And lives are given to be lived, not waited for." He stood and took his bucket and pole with him. "Just thoughts to consider." He started to leave in the direction of the docks but then, after a few steps, he turned back again. "And I did sit for a sunrise. But for you to see it, not me."

The sunrise in front of Miken was beginning to take shape. Some clouds were touched with dark blue and red while others were ripples of yellows and deep oranges. Maybe later, around midday, Miken would stroll in rain that would be light enough to lift the heat off the air. And he would try, or try as best he could, to enjoy the smell of the ocean.

Chapter 11

Hunted

After the shipwreck

Desalians. It was daybreak when Alexria first saw a handful in the forest. After their incident with the Etimire, Alexria, Lerato, and Princess Genev had moved away from their place near the evergreen. The whole area was a mess of tracks and skid marks and clawed branches. It was also likely that the Etimire had left a trail of blood from there to wherever it had dashed off to. The new location they found wasn't far. It was a cluster of cedars with a view of the ocean if the right branches were parted. Yet as helpful as that would have been to search for any approaching Hydian ships, it seemed they wouldn't be given that much time.

There were five Desalians that she and Lerato could see. One was younger than the rest, a boy no more than twenty but who held himself tall with confident authority. The other men paid close attention to the ground. It would only be a matter of time.

"Five men isn't a lot," Lerato whispered.

"There'll be more." Alexria's eyes were beyond the men, waiting for movement elsewhere in the forest.

"Then we do it quietly."

Alexria already had her bow in her hand, but she didn't reach for an arrow. They were armed men, but that wasn't her hesitation.

What slowed her was that they were unaware of the threat she posed. It felt just as low as if they had been unarmed.

"If we kill them here, their bodies will be too hard to hide," Alexria said.

"If they find us, we won't have a choice." Lerato's mind was set.

If the Desalians found them, Alexria, Lerato, and Princess Genev wouldn't be able to run. Or, rather, Lerato wouldn't be able to run. Alexria couldn't leave Lerato to have to make that choice.

Alexria picked an arrow from the quiver beside her. She set it to her bow. The man closest to her was crouched low with a hand feeling the ground. It wasn't the cold face of a Desalian that she almost hoped it would be. It was a focused face, but approachable. Approachable aside from the fact that he was among the men hunting them.

Alexria lowered her bow. "Let me lead them away from you," she said. "If they follow me, they may not realize you're here."

Lerato watched the men, but said nothing in response. Princess Genev watched Lerato with pleading eyes that he couldn't see. She looked less like the Princess seen in the Hydian corridors. Her dress and robe and sandaled feet were all scuffed with dirt from a night in the forest. Her long hair, usually well combed or styled, was windblown. Alexria knew her own appearance wasn't any better, but it was look that Alexria was comfortable with now.

"Lerato, I came with you to help keep you safe."

"You came for your own safety," Lerato corrected her.

Princess Genev finally spoke. "She's the only help you have," she said. She could barely bring her whisper loud enough to be heard. "I'm useless with a blade."

Their tracks were found. One of the guards, the one closest to them, raised a hand to signal the others. In Alexria's view, three of the Desalians were lined up in a straight shot. First the guard with his hand raised, then another guard a few strides behind him, and then a little further back, was their young commander. It was one shot that wouldn't last. With both hands already on her bow, Alexria pulled the arrow back on her bow, aimed, and released. The arrow grazed the side of the first guard, making his hand drop quickly. It also grazed the hip of the second guard. Then, instead of striking the young commander, it stopped in the tree next to his leg. It wasn't as injuring as she'd hoped. But it got their attention.

Alexria tore out of hiding among the cedars. She risked a glance back. Whether Lerato fully agreed or not, he and Princess Genev stayed hidden. It was the Desalians that were chasing after her. She didn't glance long enough to count how many. She sprinted as fast as the forest would let her. She carried a bow in one hand and she swept branches out of her way with the other. Her racing steps danced among rocks and roots and bushes. She ducked and wove among the trees. The sprint made the terrain feel more rugged, more harsh. She forced through more leaves and came into a brief clearing. She went a few strides into it, then turned and reached to her quiver for an arrow. There was none. Her hand grasped at air. She must have left her quiver back in the cedars.

The Desalians charged through the opening. Three. Alexria dropped her bow and drew her dagger. Her blade met the first man's sword as it swung up from its sheath. She blocked it and struck her fist against his cheek. He staggered back long enough for Alexria to draw a second dagger from her other boot and face the second Desalian. This man's sword was sweeping down toward her. She blocked it with her two daggers and brought her knee up hard. There was blood on his side, likely from her arrow shot earlier. She brought her elbow down into it. He flinched. She struck his wound harder. The man curled to the side in pain and, as he did, Alexria struck him on the back of the head. A boot, from the third Desalian, struck her chest and kicked her backwards. Her back fell hard into a tree. She dodged a sword coming in her direction. It grazed her shoulder with a sharp sting. Alexria regained her footing and her focus. She took a couple steps backwards to keep both men in front of her. The rest was a blur of metal and movement. Her daggers spun and slashed and blocked without her thinking. Her breaths became pants. She tried to force an opening through the Desalian's defences. As she deflected the sword of one, the second sword would already be coming toward her again.

Alexria managed to trip one of the men. As he was on the ground, Alexria caught the hilt of the second man's sword. She drove her knee up into him, threw him down past her, and, as he fell, struck the back of his head with the hilt of her dagger. A deep pain slashed at her side. Alexria gripped the pain with one hand. In a flare of strength, she turned and thrust her dagger in the direction she assumed the man to be. The blade pierced the man's shoulder, stopping him. His eyes were wide in shock. Her own eyes felt just as wide. Before he could do anything more, Alexria thrust the heel of her hand into his chin and the man dropped to the ground.

She stood there for a moment, looking at the three still men, one with her blade in his shoulder. She'd heard that it was more likely to survive such a wound if the blade was left in place until medicine was found. So she left it there.

* * * * *

Lerato wanted to call out after Alexria ran out of hiding, but that would have ruined her reason for going. He wanted to think that they'd capture her before they'd kill her. Yet even that wasn't very encouraging. It made him a coward of a Prince, was what it did. He gritted his teeth as he watched the four Desalians chase after her. One began limping from an injury on his hip and he slowed to a stop. The other three pursued Alexria until Lerato could no longer hear them in the forest. The young commander remained where he was and began scolding the limping Desalian for not seeing the archer and not being able to pursue them. The man, older and likely more experienced, returned with some authority in his own voice. The man finished with, "And if you'd consider my advice, *sir*, you'd regroup with another search part."

How many men were there out searching the forest? How many search parties?

The young commander was boiling with the urge to reply, but it seemed he had no argument.

Genev screamed as the cedar branches behind her were ripped aside. Two archers pointed ready arrows into their faces. Another Desalian Guard and another young commander, a girl this time. Lerato reached for his sword.

"Don't."

The girl's threat didn't slow him. His sword swept up, shattering the girl's arrow and slashing at the guard's wrist. The two archers fell back.

Lerato took Genev's arm and pulled her to her feet. "Go," he shouted, trying to snap the fear out of her. He felt as though he was dragging her through the cedars. "Run. Go."

There were more Desalians coming from the direction of the two archers. It was more than Lerato could take on while also protecting Genev. There were too many angles to consider. Genev was finally supporting herself on her feet.

"Find Alex. Go."

Lerato ran with her for the few strides that his aching calves would allow him to, then he let her go off on her own. At least she could run. That was more than he could do. Lerato turned to face whatever Desalians tried to chase after her. As long as Lerato drew enough attention to himself, Genev would be fine. Unless she met another search party. She couldn't meet another search party.

Lerato drew his sword. He had no time to count how many Desalians he'd be facing. It was a number likely to change. Instead he'd face the men as they came. He forced aside the first sword that swung at him and met the second sword in the same motion. He swept his sword back toward the flesh the first man, then stabbed another beside him. He ducked a new blade and noticed more Desalians coming from a different direction. As he stood a fist sent him back down. Lerato closed his eyes to shut out the throbbing of his calves. He swept his sword low around him. He only felt it catch the ankles of one man. A boot struck Lerato's side and he rolled across the ground. The end of a sword pressed against Lerato's neck and a boot stepped on his wrist. Lerato reached for his dagger with his free hand but the sword pressed harder.

"Easy, easy," said the man with the sword as though he were coaxing a horse. "Release your sword."

Lerato's chest heaved. Two men with bows aimed their arrows at his torso. He wanted to think he could draw and swing his dagger fast enough to free himself, but he resisted the reckless urge. He released his sword as ordered.

"That's better," the man said. He looked Lerato over. "Stand him up."

Two Desalians came and lifted Lerato to his feet. His arms were forced behind his back and bound before Lerato could consider resisting. The man standing before him, who had pinned him, didn't wear the same Desalian uniform as the others. He stood just as well armed, but his dark tunic was that of any common citizen.

"Adicara," the young boy commander said as he joined them, "I have men after the other two Hydians."

Though Adicara didn't smile at the news, his eyes seemed to. He stretched an arm out in the direction of Genev and Alexria. "Let's join them, shall we, your highness?"

* * * * *

Alexria took her hand away from her own injury. The side of her tunic was already stained. Her hand was painted in blood. She squeezed her hand into a fist to keep it from trembling. She had no scraps of cloth to wrap it. She had left her cloak back among the cedars. Her sleeve was already torn from the shallow cut on her shoulder so she ripped off the cloth and tried wrapping it around her waist. It wasn't long enough. Alexria closed her eyes and breathed. She gathered the cloth into ball and pressed it against her red side.

That would have to be enough to get her back to Lerato and Princess Genev.

Her bow was still on the ground near the edge of the clearing. One of the Desalian men was laying facedown and had a quiver of arrows on his back. Alexria took a handful for herself and then stopped. The strap of the quiver was sure to fit around her waist. It had to. Alexria cut one end of it, then pulled the rest of the strap out from under the man. She let the leather hold the bundle of cloth in place. Her bloody fingers fumbled with tying the strap.

A rustle of leaves came from a distance. Running. Coming closer. Alexria pulled the strap tight. Her wound complained at the pressure. She folded the leather around itself and pulled again to lock the knot. The runner clashed through the forest undergrowth nearby. Alexria fitted one of arrows to her bow, dropped to a knee, and waited for a glimpse.

The runner wasn't heading toward her. As the steps came closer it seemed the runner would pass by somewhere in the forest to her left. It also seemed there was more than one runner. The distinct steps were now blurred together in a litter of noise. She caught a glimpse of blue far off to the side. A glimpse of movement. She walked toward it, keeping herself low and an arrow pulled back on her bow. The action made her wounded side ache. There was more movement. Three Desalian men. Running. Chasing Princess Genev and gaining fast. Her pale blue cloak kept catching on undergrowth and ripping on branches, slowing her down. Alexria let an arrow fly through the only straight shot she had. Her timing missed the first guard, but it struck the legs of the second and he fell. The first guard continued after Genev. The third guard turned toward Alexria.

It took him a moment before he saw her, but when he did he came in full sprint. Alexria set another arrow to her bow. The man weaved among trees, making a difficult target. The only clear aim she had was a lethal shot to his torso. A killing shot. And even as the man drew nearer, she couldn't bring herself to loosen her grip on the arrow. She had never shot to kill. She had never killed this intentionally.

Even what she had done to the three Desalian men that lay behind her was more than she could be proud of. If she could avoid this shot, she would. Yet the ache in her side reminded her she couldn't. She didn't have the strength to fight him. Or the strength to run.

The screams of the Princess came from further off in the forest. The arrow released, aimed high, and struck the man's shoulder. Just as she did, the searing pain of a strike came to her wound. It came again. A fist pounding hard against her bloody side. Alexria keeled over in pain. Her feet were swept out from under her and she fell face down to the ground. A boot stepped on the wrist of the hand holding her bow. A knee planted into her back, knocking the wind out of her chest. Her side was throbbing. A sharp tip pushed through her hair to the back of her neck and she could hear the stretch of a bowstring being pulled back. Princess Genev could still be heard screaming and struggling.

"Move and I'll kill you," said a girl's voice from behind Alexria. There was enough strength in the words to make them believable. "By the order of my Father, Duke of Petayrn, you are under arrest. And if you value your life, you'll put your hands behind your back without a fight."

The girl's weight was more than Alexria had the strength for. The sound of Princess Genev had quieted now. It could only be hoped that the Princess had been hushed and not killed.

The Duke's daughter pressed the arrow harder into the back of Alexria's neck. "Now."

Alexria twisted one arm backwards and then the other once her wrist was freed from under the girl's boot. As quick as the girl took the arrow away, a rope was tightened around Alexria's wrists. The rope cut into her flesh enough to make her flinch. Before the girl let her up, she reached to the ground near Alexria's chin. The girl picked up the pendent of Alexria's necklace and lifted it as much as the chain would let her.

"What's this?" The girl snapped the words the way a General would. The way the Duke of Petayrn likely would.

Why would that interest her? "It has no gold value," Alexria said.

The girl dug her knee further into her back. "What is it?"

The pressure made speaking harder. She closed her eyes. "It's my daughter's."

The girl held it long enough to make Alexria fear losing it. That necklace was all she had left of her children. It was all she clung to of them. When the girl finally dropped it, Alexria let out a small breath.

"You're a thief, is what you are," the girl said. "Get up."

Chapter 12

Haunted

4 years before the shipwreck

Miken sat on the empty banquet table with one foot on the seat of a chair and the other on the armrest. He spun his dagger over and over in his hand, entertaining his restlessness. He had been informed that the Duke of Petayrn would be meeting him here, yet Miken was nearly at the point of searching for the man himself. The opening door greeted him with a surprise. It was a girl that entered, about nine or ten years old by his guess. Her dark, curly hair was done up with the elegance of royalty. Her dress, though of simple design, was made of a rich red fabric.

"My apologies, sir," the girl said.

Miken kept his dagger spinning. "You're awfully young to be a Duke."

"I am Melinda. My Father is Sular, Duke of Petayrn." She curtsied low. "Unless I was too young to remember, I don't believe we've met."

"I don't believe we have." It had been years since he had last been allowed ashore this island. His last visit may even had been before Melinda was born. Or close to it. Miken sheathed the dagger and climbed down from the table. He felt as though he towered over her.

"I'm told you are Miken, Ambassador for the people, reporting to the King himself."

Miken let out a small, amused smile. It was common for Desalian children to grow up quickly, especially children of powerful men. Yet Miken rarely spent time with such children. Their maturity was little more than a mask.

"Can I expect your father anytime soon?"

"He's gone out to observe the island," Melinda said. "As we speak, he's being informed of your arrival."

"And your brothers?"

"My brother and sister are travelling with him."

Miken caught the word 'sister' and thought of Allia, as he always seemed to do. He held back the temptation to ask about her. He couldn't sound too urgent. He couldn't raise suspicions. "Well, if I must wait," he said, "perhaps you could tour me your fortress. It has been a long time since I've been here."

Melinda smiled. She swept a wide arm toward the doors. "Of course, sir. This way."

Miken followed her. He observed most of the fortress from the highest point of it, a deep ledge on the mountain face. From there, Melinda pointed out the secure structure of the fortress built against the mountain, the moat which met up with the ocean itself, the farming villages, the forest, the docks, and the collection of ships which was small compared to numbers they had roaming the waters. All the while Miken waited, almost painfully, for her to mention her sister again. It wasn't until she pointed out a riding party coming toward the fortress that she did at last. 'The twins' was what she called them.

"How old are the twins now?"

"Fourteen," Melinda said. "Four years older than myself."

Allia would be thirteen. It was close enough. "My memory of Petayrn must not be as good as I thought it to be," Miken said. "I seem to remember both twins being boys." He was certain of this fact. He would remember a girl that close to Allia's age. He only hoped his question sounded innocent enough.

"It has always been Sinele and Melony," she said. "As long as I can remember."

Melony. The name would have come from Duke Sular's wife, the same way Allia's name had come from Alexria.

Yet hearing of her and meeting her were two very different tasks to endure. Duke Sular introduced them as Sinele, his son and heir, and Melony, his daughter. Both true Desalians. They were both dressed like Duke Sular with clean riding attire, boots, and a sword at their sides. Miken did his best not to gaze too long at Melony. Her hair was dark enough to be compared to theirs, as was her complexion. However she lacked the curls that Sular, Sinele, and Melinda all shared.

Miken greeted Sinele by saying, "I look forward to seeing you become the Duke you'll grow to be."

To Melony, who greeted him with a respectful nod instead of curtsy, he said, "I'll assume you have your mother's beauty." He was looking at Alexria. Her eyes, her nose, the smooth line of her jaw. Melony had it all.

Her smile looked forced. She wasn't the type to aim for such compliments. "Thank-you, sir," she said. "That's what I'm told."

Of course she was.

* * * * *

Miken didn't stay long on Petayrn. He'd likely kill Duke Sular if he did. It took all the patience Miken had to listen to Sular talk through the political and military business of his island. Sular tried to have his 'twins,' Sinele and Melony, join for the conversation, but Miken didn't allow it. Who was Sular to claim Allia as Melony? Did he think no one would notice or no one would find out? There were several times that Miken wished he could reach over the table and strangle the man where he sat. But he couldn't justify the action. News would spread fast through Desali that the Ambassador killed a Duke without cause. Miken would be named a traitor, which was a death-sentence for a Desalian. So Miken left at the earliest chance he could.

Before Miken could reach his ship off Petayrn, a woman met him on one of the passages. The shawl over her hair and plain dress labeled her as a servant.

"May we speak, sir," she said. Her foreign accent meant she was a servant bought from some other kingdom. Perhaps Rylan.

"Make it quick." Miken kept walking, forcing her to follow.

Her accent was strong and she had difficulty finding all the words she needed. "For long time I have waited to see man look at her as you do," the servant said.

Though curious, Miken didn't slow his pace. "Who do I look at?"

The servant had a gentle voice. "You miss her. As a father should."

Before Miken could stop himself, he turned, took the servant's neck in his hand, and pushed her against the passage wall. "Those are dangerous words," he said in a hiss.

Though Miken had a hand ready to slap over her mouth, she didn't cry out in pain or fear. Though she'd closed her eyes as she struck the wall, when she opened them again her gaze was calm, maybe even sad.

"You are in pain," she said.

"Tell me what you know and say it quick," Miken said quietly.

"You know same I do," the servant said. "You see truth. Your heart show you it." She put a hand on his chest as she said the word 'heart.'

Miken couldn't fill in the gaps himself. He couldn't risk saying it. "What truth?"

"I raise children of Duke."

"From birth?" He needed her to say it. He needed someone, anyone else, to say it.

Her sad eyes were searching his, as though she could see what he wanted. "I first come and heal Sinele when he fell ill, I raise Melinda from birth, and I raise Melony from when she arrive here."

Miken finally released the woman. He paced the width of the hall. He thought it'd be easier to hear than that. He thought it'd lighten the burden of seeing Allia here. Instead the words had worsened it. He couldn't deny it now. He couldn't pretend it was just a hopeful trick of his mind.

"I see now," the woman said, "Melony has eyes of her father, not of Sular."

Miken sharply turned back to her. "Why didn't you tell her? You knew the truth. You knew who she was. You could have freed her from this."

"Her story is not mine to tell," the woman said.

The calmness in her voice only frustrated him more.

"Hearing and trusting are both different," the woman said. "You know that more than me."

Miken leaned back against the opposite wall, defeated. He did know that. He knew that all too well.

* * * * *

It was evening of the day Miken had promised to return. So when there was still no sign of him, that was enough to concern Lerato. Alexria hadn't shown any sign of worry yet. Last Lerato saw her, she was walking the Hydian halls with Lady Samila. Alexria was making a habit of talking with Lady Samila during her visits. The talks seemed to be good for her. She looked lighter and more refreshed afterwards. So if Alexria had any worries now, Lady Samila would be best to calm them.

As for Lerato, he continually caught himself looking into crowds or down passages with the hopes of seeing Miken. It was as he walked the fortress wall with Kaytan that his eyes were drawn to a certain crowd. The Western Gate was the only one of four that had no houses outside it, and so it was here that citizen's often gathered as an informal training arena. Even the grass had been worn away into a ring of dirt. It was here a crowd had gathered. The crowd had arranged into a ring themselves, leaving the middle open for two sparing men. Though the faces were difficult to see from where Lerato stood on the wall, he could recognize one of the sparing men as Miken.

"I'm told they've been there all evening," Kaytan said.

Miken won his match with quick, sure strokes of this sparing pole. He was fighting hard against the men, harder than Lerato had seen him spare with Alexria, and he was finishing each match quickly. Still, after each man fell, there always seemed to be another ready face Miken next.

As far as Lerato was aware, it wasn't Miken's way to not return directly to Alexria. It wasn't his way to delay this much. So what was the man trying to accomplish?

"I need an unofficial favour," Lerato said.

Kaytan grinned. "You still know how to catch my interest."

Lerato turned his back on the distant crowd, as though that would somehow conceal his thoughts from them. "How soon can you have ten archers on this wall and casually ready to take aim?"

"Casually?" Kaytan said, catching the word. He took a long look at the rough men of the crowd and then back to Lerato. "Let me come with you."

"It's for personal reasons."

"You're father won't like the idea."

That was true. Lerato's father was a cautious King. Unlike Lady Samila, he preferred not to mingle much with the common citizen's. This was especially so with rough men like those Lerato planned to walk into.

"I know you don't either," Lerato said. "But between a Prince and a General, it's hard to say who has the higher authority in this case."

"Hm," Kaytan said with a smirk. "It's hard to say who's more reckless, too, but somehow that's rarely a factor in our discussions."

"Good," Lerato said, slapping Kaytan's shoulder and turning to leave. "I'm sure you'll keep an eye on me."

Kaytan made no further objection, assuring Lerato that the decision was made.

By the time Lerato reached the Western Gate, the number of men on the wall had already doubled. Kaytan had gathered more than ten archers, a comforting fact. As Lerato neared the crowd he noticed that their noise was not as much cheers as it was commentary. They'd applaud, laugh, point, and cringe, yet there was no continuous shouting to encourage a win by either side. It was a different setting from the tournaments Lerato had witnessed over the years. The setting was more rough. It wasn't the place to excuse himself as he pushed through the crowd.

Lerato reached the front row as a new match was beginning. Miken glistened with sweat and his drenched shirt lay on the ground near him. Yet there was still strength in him. His eyes burned like fire as he faced his opponent. The opponent was of similar stature and size. Miken didn't wait for the man to lead the fight. Miken made all the attacking strikes, forcing the man into a frantic defensive. Miken never paused long enough to offer the man a weak opening to strike at. Before the man could consider sweating, his legs were swept up by Miken's sparing pole and a hit from Miken's elbow kept the man on the ground.

Miken picked up the man's sparing pole and waited as the man staggered out of the arena. Miken used the time to settle his heaving chest. Various men in the crowd began raising their hands and shouting challenges. Miken circled, eyeing each of them and holding the sparing poles ready. When his gaze reached Lerato he paused. Lerato raised a casual hand before he could stop himself. This hadn't been part of his intentions.

Miken let out a light scoff. "You wouldn't survive this kind of arena."

Lerato took more offense to the words than he thought he would. "I'll argue that."

Miken still wore an amused smile. "I'm not fighting you." He tossed the pole toward a man near Lerato whose hand had been raised.

Lerato caught it. The action sparked a murmur of oh's and chuckles from the crowd. The man who had been tossed the pole tried to snatch it back. When Lerato's grip held it, the man struck him hard across the face.

"Gentlemen," Miken's voice raised over the crowd.

The man that had struck Lerato paused. Miken held his hand high to gain the crowd's fading attention. The noise settled enough for Miken to be heard and listened to as though Miken were their General.

"Humour me, if you will," Miken said, "but it seems we've found a lost kitten."

"In an Etimire pack," added a voice in the crowd.

The men chuckled. Even Miken widened his odd smile.

"Now what good is a kitten within an Etimire pack?" Miken paced the circle with his confident gaze challenging the men. "Hm?"

"As good as bait, I'd say," one man answered.

The words prompted laughter.

Miken looked at Lerato. "As good as bait," he said slowly.

Lerato's security suddenly felt as though it had been a false sense of it. He considered signalling to Kaytan on the fortress wall, yet wondered how he was to do that.

"Now if you'd excuse me," Miken said, "I should return the kitten to its pen." His expression was still one of amusement, entertaining the crowd. "I'd hate for the dogs to have to fetch it."

Miken picked up his shirt and tossed his own pole to someone else in the circle. He walked past Lerato and took his arm in a firm grip. Miken pushed their way through the crowd, only releasing Lerato after they were out of it. They headed toward the Western Gate.

"You'll get yourself killed one of these days," Miken said once they were far enough away from the men. His crowd-entertaining tone had vanished. "And it should have been today."

The accusation felt harsh. "The Hydian General himself was ready to coordinate a strike if it came to that."

"You mean the handful of men on the wall?"

Lerato didn't think it had been that obvious.

Miken went on. "Archers are useless if you're already dead. And considering there were more Desalians in that crowd then I could point out, some men were very ready to do it."

The thought made Lerato's stomach feel unsettled. He had the urge to look back at the men, but didn't want to bring that much attention to himself. "Who are you to them?" Lerato asked.

"Respected enough to keep them off you," Miken said.

"I noticed." Lerato felt more frustrated with him than anything else. "Then at least tell me why you haven't already gone to Alex."

"It's complicated."

They had passed through the Western Gate by now, making Lerato less hesitant to motion toward the crowd. "What happened back there was complicated," he said.

"What happened back there was your mistake, not mine." Miken turned to go back to the men they had just left.

Lerato grabbed his arm. Miken ripped it away.

"Where are you going?" Lerato demanded.

"I'm not coming back."

The statement felt blunt. Did he mean to Alexria? Lerato caught up to him and stood in his path. When Miken tried to keep going, Lerato barred him with a hand on Miken's chest.

"Then what do I tell Alex?" Lerato asked, his voice hushed to keep the conversation more between them.

"The truth."

"Which is what?"

"She's safer without me." His eyes dared Lerato to challenge the words.

Lerato allowed the heat in his voice to settle. "What happened to you and Alex, to your children, was *years* ago. She's been safe with you since then." He whispered this. He was sure no one else knew of the incident. Lerato had certainly never mentioned it. Alexria seemed even less likely to speak of what happened. "Hasn't she?"

Miken looked at him for a long time. The tense muscles in his jaw loosened. "What would you do," he asked, "if you learned a secret that would break your wife's heart? What would you do if she deserved to know?"

Lerato's eyes flinched in thought. "That's not an easy question." Complicated was the word that he wanted to use. That seemed to describe so much of Miken and Alexria. "Whether you choose to tell her or not, you shouldn't run from her."

"I shouldn't do a lot of things."

"And I know that's never stopped you before." Lerato took his hand off him. For the moment, Miken seemed capable of staying where he was.

Miken shifted his weight. The strength of his expression and stature was weakening. "I need you to look after Alex from now on."

"I can't do that."

"You need to do that."

Lerato shook his head. "I won't be able to keep her here."

"Where would she want to go?"

"After *you*." How could he be so blind to that? "Because that's what you do when someone you love is out of your reach. You do everything you can to find them again."

Miken's mouth and chin twitched, maybe even trembled. Then he tightened his jaw, breathed, and the trembling stopped. "What if when you find them, it's already too late. Do you just walk away?"

There was more to that than Lerato knew. It was complicated. He could see that much. "Right now," Lerato said as carefully as he could, "you need to go to her. Start with that."

Miken had nothing else to snap back with. His gaze struggled to hold to Lerato's. When Miken finally looked away, he turned. This time he went in the direction of Alexria.

Chapter 13

Masked Stories

After the shipwreck

Alexria stared at the ground as she waited on her knees. She focused on breathing deep. In and out. It didn't help ease the throbbing of her wounded side, but it was likely the best thing for her to do. She couldn't press her hand against her side anymore. Her hands were bound behind her back instead and a Desalian stood guard near her to be sure she stayed that way. Princess Genev knelt next to her, also bound but so far unharmed. The Princess whimpered though, as if she did have some kind of injury. It was likely she imagined the prisons waiting for them. Alexria couldn't afford those kinds of thoughts. She had to keep herself calm. She had to keep her heart slow to keep the bleeding of her wound slow. At least, that was what she told herself. She could feel blood dripping down her arm from the cut on her shoulder and she was glad that wound was shallow instead.

There were only two Desalians with them. One was the Desalian man that had caught Princess Genev. The other was the young commander, the girl that had caught Alexria. The young commander paced back and forth across the forest floor. Alexria listened to the rhythm of her steps to help the time pass.

More footsteps soon joined hers and could be heard approaching them. It was a group of several Desalians. Lerato was among them with his hands bound as well. When the girl greeted the man in front as "Adicara," Alexria found herself skip a breath. After all this time, the man was finally standing in front of her. Everything about him was strong. His stature, his face, his stride, his confidence. Alexria had told herself she wouldn't be intimidated by him anymore, but how could she? She was weak and broken. He wasn't.

Lerato was stopped a few strides away Alexria and the Princess. A blade hovered near his neck in the hands of a Desalian to keep him in his place. Adicara, after speaking briefly to the girl, was the one who came to them instead. He crouched in front of them.

"The royal lady," Adicara had said, taking Princess Genev's chin in his grip. "I trust your bonds are comfortable."

The Princess only trembled. This was the same man she had spoken to while on board the ship, the man she had trusted.

Adicara smirked and let her go before looking at Alexria. "Now, who did you drag along with you?"

Lerato spoke up then from where he stood. "She's a maid."

Adicara raised his eyebrows curiously. "Only a maid?"

His reaction made her wonder if he knew otherwise. It didn't make sense for him to remember her. That night had been a long time ago and the room had been dim.

Alexria made herself nod and she swallowed back her pain so she could speak. "I'm a maid to the lady."

Adicara studied her face for a moment and then shifted closer toward her. He put one hand on the back of her neck and moved close to her ear. He put his other hand on her side and she groaned. Alexria closed her eyes as though that would shut away the pain. Her breaths sharpened.

When Adicara spoke it was in a whisper meant only for her. "I'm curious, Alex, about what Miken would do to a maid in Desali."

* * * * *

The walk to the fortress with bound hands should have dampened his pride. Likely that was what the walk was meant to accomplish. Instead Lerato could feel himself fuming. If it weren't for his hands behind his back, he would have been waiting for a chance to strike whichever Desalian tried taunting him first.

Lerato was forced down to his knees. He refused flinching at the hard impact of the floor. Genev stumbled to her knees on one side of him and Alexria on the other side. Of the three of them, Alexria dropped the lowest and she was slow to straighten herself up. Even when she did she kept her head down, with loose strands of hair hiding her face, and her shoulders were curled over. There was pain in her heavy, controlled breaths. In Genev, there was fear in her stiff and trembling frame. If it weren't for the ropes binding all their hands and the Desalians guarding them, Lerato would have tried to tend to them both. But that wasn't possible here in the Desalian fortress on Petayrn. They had been brought into the banquet hall, which seemed an odd place to bring prisoners, but it was where they met the man that appeared to be in charge. The man, Duke Sular according to what Lerato had overheard, was pacing the room when they arrived, waiting for them.

"Adicara?" the Duke asked, looking to the men behind Lerato for an explanation.

"You're prize, as promised," Adicara said. "Lerato, the Hydian Prince, and his sister, Princess Genev."

A whip snapped against Lerato's back and he groaned at the unexpected pain. Genev let out a yelp of pain of her own.

The Duke looked at Alexria. "And?"

The whip snapped against Alexria. She made less noise than Lerato had. She swallowed the pain. Her head dropped lower. Her next several breaths trembled.

"By her word," Adicara said, "she is a maid. By my eye, I'd say she's well trained with a bow."

At the word 'maid,' the Duke appeared uninterested. He took a chair from the banquet table and slid it in front of Lerato. "You'll have to forgive my son's whip," he said as he sat. "It's his newest trick."

Lerato assumed the Duke's son to be the young commander called Sinele. He could picture Sinele's harsh nature at the whip's handle. Despite how young the boy was, Lerato had no sympathy for him. He was plenty old enough to be accountable for his actions.

"I'll have to admit," the Duke said, "I almost didn't believe the rumours that royalty had been on board the ship. I would have been satisfied with the net-full of Hydians we already have waiting for you."

The echo of distant boots came from the long hall that Lerato, Genev, and Alexria had just walked up. The Duke's eyes glanced toward the sound as he spoke.

"Thirty-six Hydians should earn me decent bartering leverage," the Duke said. He waved a hand toward Alexria. "Or should I say thirty-seven. And as much as I'd like to barter the Hydian Royalty myself, I don't believe I'll have the privilege of deciding your fate." He glanced past Lerato again. The walking boots were closer. "I'm forced to remember how quickly news travels among the Desali Islands. And my authority is about to be replaced."

"Good," Lerato said, keeping his words sharp. "I'd rather speak to the King than a Duke."

His comment was met with another sting of the whip.

The Duke shrugged. Either he didn't take offense to the words or he saw the whip's retaliation to be effective enough. "Not quite the King, yet his brother should be close enough to satisfy you."

"Sular," came the new voice from the hall, "do yourself a favour and get out of that chair. It makes you look weak."

The authority of the voice was clear and Duke Sular responded to it by standing and stepping aside. But, more than that, the voice was hauntingly familiar. As soon as the Duke was out of the way, a cloak was tossed over Lerato's head and landed in a heap on the chair.

"And I hope what you dragged me up here to see is better than the useless sailors I found in your prison."

It was Miken. His very presence in the room made the guards stand straighter at attention. If there was an image Lerato had of how a Desalian should look, Miken fit it. Lerato could feel himself heating.

Miken strode into their view and circled to look at their faces. He was close enough to reach them if he'd wanted. He paused and let out a sigh. "Sular, you continue to surprise me," he said.

Lerato spoke up. "Your brother is the King?" Miken had never even hinted toward having that much authority in Desali.

"'Ambassador' is preferred," Miken said casually. "'Brother' implies friendship."

Lerato could only shake his head. "I trusted you." Even to himself the words sounded pathetic, but those were the only words he could fit together at first.

Miken gave him an entertained smile. "I know you did." He turned his attention to the Duke.

"*She* trusted you."

Miken held up a finger as he looked back at Lerato. "The men are talking," he said as though coaxing a child. "Besides, the Lady doesn't look nearly as eager to share her disappointment as you do."

The Lady? Did he think he referred to Genev? How could Miken not recognize Alexria next to them. "She at least deserves-"

A swing from Miken's backhand interrupted Lerato. It stung Lerato's face and nearly knocked him over. He wanted to think this was the second time Miken had ever hit him. Yet the first time had been different from this one. The first time had been forgivable.

"What do you hope to accomplish by killing them?" Miken asked the Duke.

"I don't plan to, Sir."

"You mean to barter with them?" Miken scoffed and turned. "Lerato, my friend, how long have we known each other."

"Too long."

The breath of a whip could be heard readying to swing. Lerato stiffened, bracing himself for it.

"Sinele," Miken said before the strike came. "I believe I can handle Hydian prisoners without your help. Now I suggest you put that down before you tangle yourself up in it." His casual tone had a subtle bite in the words.

After a moment's pause, Sinele could be heard moving to the side of the room.

Miken continued. "A number, Lerato. How many years have I known you?"

"Fifteen." The number was only an estimate. If anyone knew the accurate answer, it would be Miken and Alexria. Yet neither of them seemed available to ask.

Miken turned back to the Duke. "I've spent fifteen years gaining their trust. Now the moment they walk back into the Hydian Capital, my face will be on every Wanted poster in the kingdom."

"There's a quick solution to that." The voice came from behind Lerato.

The Duke motioned toward the voice as he took a retreating step backwards. "May I introduce Adicara, the bounty hunter who arranged the capture."

"Adicara." Miken's chin tipped up slightly as he studied the man. Adicara must have been standing in a place where Miken couldn't notice him at first. "I believe we've met."

"I believe we have," Adicara said. "Once."

Miken casually adjusted his stance to a wide, sturdy one. "I hear quick solutions are a specialty of yours."

"In this case, that solution is a Royal Hydian Lady by the name Lacina."

Lerato's stomach turned with knots at the mention of his wife's name. "You touch her, I'll kill you both."

Yet Adicara had stolen all of Miken's attention.

"Too much knowledge can be a dangerous thing in Desali," Miken said.

"It can also be profitable."

"And what is your profitable plan for these three?"

"I've already made my profit from the Duke."

"And yet you're still here."

"Curiosity."

Lerato was tempted to turn and see Adicara. He pictured the man to now be a mirror of Miken: cool composure supported by defensive strength. Any true emotion shrouded in a rehearsed mask.

"I'll admit I'm most curious about the maid," said Adicara.

Lerato had noticed Adicara take brief interest in Alexria while they had been in the forest. Adicara had whispered something to her. He had leaned close to her ear to say it as though it were a secret between them. Lerato had wanted to read her face. Yet when Adicara had put a hand on her wounded side, all her face wore was pain.

"This maid?" Miken asked. He finally turned toward Alexria.

Until then, Alexria had kept still and quiet. Her head remained down with loose strands of her hair shielding her face from the room. Her breaths had settled somewhat in that time, but were still heavy. Lerato almost expected Miken to grab her hair and wrench her head back to look at him. But he didn't. Instead Miken reached a slow hand out and touched Alexria's chin.

"Look at me, girl," Miken said.

She did. Alexria tipped her head up slowly, as though she feared the movement itself would worsen her pain. As her hair dropped away like a curtain it revealed a dirty and damp face. Lerato hoped it was damp from sweat. He couldn't bear to think it was from tears. Alexria closed her eyes and when she opened them again she had lifted her gaze to meet Miken's. There was no change to Miken's expression. He looked her over as though she had been any other woman. Lerato wanted to strike some sense into him.

"Whoever she is, you've broken her," Miken said.

Lerato blinked. Miken was protecting her. The only way he knew how. As the Hydian Prince and Princess, they couldn't hide in Desali territory. Alexria could. To the Desalians, she had to be no one.

"If I was broken, you'd know it," Alexria said.

Her strength surprised Lerato. There was still fatigue in the curl of her shoulders and pain in the lines of her face, yet she had found enough strength to put in her voice.

Miken looked her over again. "Then I'd hate to see what it'd take to break you."

He was about to turn away from her when Alexria added, "The last time Hydian Royalty was taken captive, it was the Guardians of Hydia that freed them. You should expect that to happen again."

Miken's amused expression returned. "Should I?"

"The Guardian's of Hydia are long dead," Adicara said from behind them.

"Unfortunate, but true," Miken said without sympathy. He turned to Genev, keeping a patient hand on Alexria's chin. "My Lady."

Genev flinched as though she had been startled.

"How long has it been since the Guardian's of Hydia needed to rescue their own Royalty?" Miken asked.

Genev swallowed. She trembled more than Alexria, and it wasn't from pain. Genev had been fortunate enough to remain relatively unharmed until now.

"Don't hide your tongue, my Lady," Miken said, "I know it's fluent."

Genev looked at the ground as she spoke, reciting what she knew well. "A generation-and-a-half ago the Hydian Capital was taken under Desalian control," she said. "The King was killed and the Prince, our Father, was young enough to be spared. It was the Guardians of Hydia who led the attack that drove the Desalians out. The last of the Guardians of Hydia, Arimon, was killed while we were too young to remember him."

Miken looked back at Alexria, satisfied. "Now which Guardian of Hydia were you hoping would come for you?"

Alexria didn't seem to have an answer, but she didn't turn her gaze the way Genev would have.

"The new ones," Lerato said. He had to take the attention off of Alexria.

"The new ones?" Miken asked.

"You're a knowledgeable man," Lerato said, imitating the mocking tone he had heard from Miken. "I'm sure you heard the rumours."

"I'm the ear of the King. All I ever hear are rumours," Miken said. "And all that ever comes of them are false hopes, stabbed backs, and bloody gold. My assumption for your rumour is false hope."

A girl entered the room from one of the side doorways. She was the other young commander that Lerato had seen in the forest. Her stride had a purpose to it. "We need to talk."

She gained all the eyes in the room. Miken took his hand from Alexria's chin.

It was the Duke that answered her. "Melony, this isn't the time."

"We need to talk about *her*," Melony said, pointing a harsh finger at Alexria. "I want to know who she is."

"She's a Hydian maid," the Duke said. His tone was surprisingly calm compared to the girl's.

Melony had reached them now. "Then why does she have this." She slammed an open hand on the table, leaving something behind as she did. All Lerato could see was a small chain fall onto the table.

Duke Sular picked it up and studied the pendent of the necklace. "This is yours," he said.

"Then why does she wear the *exact* same one?" Melony didn't seem to care about the additional audience of Miken and Adicara and the other guards in the room. To her there was only herself, Duke Sular, and Alexria.

The Duke brought the necklace to Alexria, whose eyes were down again. He reached for her neck, found the pendent of the necklace she wore, and brought it out into his view. Lerato couldn't see much from where he was. He had barely noticed Alexria's necklace himself. He knew she wore one. That much he could remember, but he couldn't even recall what it looked like.

The Duke released Alexria's necklace, then took her hair and tipped her face up to look at him. The sudden movement made Alexria wince in pain. Miken stood off to the side watching. His arrogant expression had faded back into one of observation. He said nothing during the time spent by the Duke studying Alexria's face. There was a brief moment when Miken's gaze drifted over to Lerato, then returned to watching Sular and Alexria. Miken's mask was weakening.

"Sinele," the Duke said finally as he continued to study Alexria, "see to it that these Hydians are brought to the cell with the others."

He took Alexria by the arm and lifted her to her feet. He ignored her soft groan of pain. Other Desalians lifted Lerato and Genev. Sinele began escorting them out with rough shoves to get them moving. Adicara left ahead of them.

"I apologize for my daughter, Sir," Duke Sular said to Miken, "but I also need everyone else to leave."

Miken and the Duke were behind them now, but they were still close enough to be heard.

"Be sure to remind your daughter of the art of interruption," Miken said.

"I assure you, Sir, I will."

As Lerato was led down the stone passage, he heard the solid banquet hall doors close.

* * * * *

Miken couldn't hear anything through the doors. He wished he could. He wished he could know how Duke Sular chose to answer Melony's demands. Chances were, the answers would be as shallow as possible. Sular was a weak Duke with a small island to govern. He couldn't afford to have even his 'daughter' turn against him. But if the girl was looking for answers, she was stubborn enough to seek them out. So why not tell her himself? Miken wouldn't tell her everything.

He couldn't tell her everything. Yet perhaps he could tell her just enough to keep her satisfied and just enough to keep her from doing anything irrational.

The door opened, hiding Miken behind it, and Melony walked through on her own. Miken pushed his hand against the door and hoped the soft thud of it closing would make her turn. When it didn't, he called her name. It startled her and she stopped mid-stride.

When she noticed him, she settled her hands respectfully behind her back. "I need to apologize to you for my behaviour," Melony said.

"Those are Sular's words," Miken said as he started toward her. She had covered a good distance in a short time. "And I think what you *need* is answers."

"The necklace is a useless trinket," Melony said, showing him that she still carried it in her hand. "It's one of hundred's made."

Miken held out his hand. Melony hesitated, then gave the necklace to him.

"Is that what he told you?" Miken said. He walked past her so Melony would have to follow.

"My father bought it from a merchant sailor," she said. "I'd cling to it for days at a time when I was young. They couldn't get it out of my hand."

Miken believed the story of her clinging to it was true. He could remember seeing Allia often reach for Alexria's necklace. It explained how this little pendent had survived the journey to the Desali islands all those years ago.

"You believe all that?" Miken asked.

She looked at him. "Why would my father lie to me?"

Miken sighed. "Melony," he said, dangling the necklace out for her to take back, "you should have realized by now that every Desalian man lives and lies to protect himself. That includes Sular, Sinele, Adicara... even me."

"Then why should I believe anything you tell me?"

Miken smiled at her comment. It proved the point he was about to make. "Because, unlike Sular, you're smart enough to figure out when you're being played. You can't figure out how right now, but you know that you are."

They reached a cross-roads in the hall where the passage stretched for a long distance to the left and the right. Miken stopped here and stood in a place where he had a view of all three directions.

"So, what's your story?" She faced him squarely, looking for a direct answer. His authority didn't seem to intimidate her. She'd grow to be a dangerous Desalian.

"You've heard of the plague?"

"Sinele and I survived it when we were young."

Miken leaned back against the wall and folded his arms. "If it killed half of the young children in Desali, how did the children of nearly every man in power remain untouched."

Melony needed a slight pause before she could answer. "They could afford the medicine."

"No known cure was found."

She had no response. "Then how else would you explain it?"

He couldn't just tell her. She wouldn't believe him if he did that. She'd have no reason to believe him anyway. But that's not what he needed her to do. He needed Melony to think. She needed to ask questions and have doubts and challenge the very kingdom she was loyal to. If he could accomplish that much with Melony, maybe he could do the same with other young Desalians who survived the plague. Maybe this would be how kingdom of Desali would tear itself apart from the inside. It's come close to happening before. The distrust among the men in power was Desali's greatest weakness.

"Why don't you look like your brother?" Miken asked.

She studied him for a moment. She seemed more doubtful of the question than her answer. "Not all twins look exactly the same."

"He looks far more like your sister than you."

"Sinele and Melinda look more like our father. I look more like our mother."

Sular must have already prepared her for such questions. "How old is Sinele?" Miken asked.

"Nineteen."

"And how old are you?"

"We're twins."

"How old are you?" Miken asked again.

Her jaw was tightening in the same way Miken's did when he became irritated. "Nineteen. Why does it matter?"

"Why are you smaller than him?" Miken asked, feeding her frustration.

"I'm not smaller," she snapped back.

"I'm not saying you are," Miken said. He kept his voice patient. "I'm saying you're younger. At least by a year." She was seventeen and a half, to be exact. But telling her that would reveal too much about himself.

She glared at him. "I'm not a Hydian maid's daughter." She had put together enough of the pieces to figure out what he was saying.

"You have Desalian blood," Miken said in a partial attempt to assure her. "You've convinced me of that. But I'd wager that blood isn't Sular's."

If she were anything like Miken, she'd be wanting to relieve her anger with her fist. Miken's authority was likely the reason she didn't. "You're right," she said. "I'm smart enough to know when I'm being played." She walked past him.

"Sular's not the only Desalian who did it," Miken said as she walked away. "I could name several other examples."

"Did you do it?" Melony asked, turning sharply back to face him. "Did you claim the son of a sailor? Or a blacksmith? Or the Desalian neighbour next to you?"

The truth seemed an appropriate answer for this question. "The plague took my children from me." The words sounded cold.

"Then why not replace them, like everyone else did?" Melony asked.

Miken took a step toward her. "Because a King needs an Heir. A Duke and a General needs an Heir. The King's brother doesn't. I had no need to replace the lost honour."

Melony shook her head. "I'm glad for your children," she said without sympathy. "They're better off dead than having a liar as a father."

With that, she left him. Miken let her go. He felt as though her words should have hurt him. Maybe a few years ago it would have when he first found her. But by now he could see that she wasn't his little girl anymore. She wasn't the young woman he had imagined she'd grow up to be. She was no different from any other born and raised Desalian. She was more like himself than Alexria. And whether Melony knew it or not, Miken would use her to turn the kingdom of Desali against itself again. All he had done now was plant the seed. That was all he needed to do now. Perhaps on his next visit he would check to see how that seed had sprouted. But until then, with Melony now out of the way, Miken's focus was Alexria. He had more chance of saving her than he did Melony.

Miken turned down the hall in the opposite direction that Melony had gone in. A medicine woman lived in the fortress. She raised Sular's children from birth and raised Melony since she had been brought here. If there was any medicine on this island that could help Alexria, this woman would have it. Miken found it difficult to keep his steps from rushing. He kept a strong stride, but held himself back from doing anything more than that. He couldn't draw unnecessary attention and curious questions.

The medicine woman's quarters were fairly close to the banquet hall. The door was open. The room was lined with plants of all kinds, some green and some flowering. There was also a tall shelf filled with vials, basins, jars, cloths, and dried leaves. Of everything here, there had to be something for Alexria.

"I thought you would come," the woman said as she rose from a simple chair. Her foreign accent was strong as it always seemed to be. Yet Miken had learned she was intelligent despite her struggled voice and missing words. "Melony say little when she search for a necklace, but she say enough."

This woman had become one that intrigued him. Not only did she listen carefully, which most servants did more than they'd admit to, but she could also piece together even the most distant pieces of information. Miken could never decide if this skill was from knowledge or intuition. Or both. Regardless, he didn't have the time to ask.

Miken closed the door. "I need something for a serious flesh wound," he said.

"It is here already," she said. She walked to where a jar, a vile, and a cloth sat together on a table. Miken's question must have been clear in his face because she added, "Melony say she found woman with her necklace. She speak of battle and of injury."

At least there was some reasoning to the woman's assumptions. "How do I use it?" he asked.

The woman handed him the jar and cloth first. The liquid in the jar was the pale brown colour of tea. "This is the Balus Root in most pure form," she said. "This will cause her great pain and great healing."

Miken didn't know there was a pure form of the Balus Root. The powder he was familiar with stung enough on its own.

The woman handed him the vile. "This will bring her strength for short time only. She take this before you leave with her."

Miken slowly took it. "You're assuming I'd help Hydians escape," he said, but maintaining his careless act was hard to do with her. She seemed to know too much. She seemed to see too much.

"If she wear the necklace, she is your daughter's mother," she said. "She is your wife."

Hearing that while standing on Desali territory sent chills down his spine. Those were dangerous words to speak in a place like this. The closed door was his only hope that no one else had heard them.

The woman touched a soft hand to his shoulder. "You leave with her."

Chapter 14

Evening Dancing

4 years before the shipwreck

The evening was dragging on. Alexria had watched the morning brighten from one of the fortress gardens. She'd hoped Miken would be returning early from Desali this time. She'd spent a lot of time talking with Lady Samila and there were many things she wanted to share with him. They had spoken of the old Guardians of Hydia and how they also began as common men. They spoke of the Citizen's Tournament where Alexria had first caught the eye of Lady Samila. Lady Samila spoke of her first days in Hydia, ten generations ago, how she chose to stay with the Hydian people and built her respect among them. Alexria spoke of her children. It surprised her at first that she had been able to, that she could speak of their childhood without being overcome with emotion. It made Lady Samila smile to hear such stories. When Alexria spoke of Allia she mentioned that sometimes, not often, but sometimes, she'd wonder if her little girl was still alive.

"That thought used to eat at me," Alexria had said. "I can't let myself think like that anymore."

"Only faith can truly counter fear," Lady Samila had said.

"Faith in what?" Alexria asked.

A soft breeze had floated past them then. It made the curtains of Lady Samila's quarters sway in and out.

"Faith, child, that the Greater Power has never abandoned you," Lady Samila said. "Neither has He abandoned your daughter."

Alexria had heard the Greater Power mentioned before from others. She could also remember it vaguely from her own childhood, but it had been so long since she'd thought of it herself. "I don't know what that means."

Lady Samila smiled in the gentle way she always did. "The Greater Power is He who has always protected you and guided you toward the right path. It is He who gave you your first breath in this world. It is also He who will guide your last breath home."

She remembered. It had been a long time since she'd heard those words but she could remember being told the same ones.

"Alexria," Lady Samila said, taking Alexria's hands in hers. "Child, whether your daughter lives or not, know that she is safe in the Greater Power's arms. Know also that if it is meant for your paths to cross, they will."

It was all this that Alexria wanted to tell Miken the most. But she didn't know how to tell him without mentioning their children. It was something they didn't speak of. It was easier that way. Easier to move past it that way.

But now as Alexria sat in her quarters, watching evening slowly darken it, she thought less of what she wanted to tell Miken and more about when he'd be coming back. Alexria held the pendent of her necklace between her fingers, sliding it back and forth along the chain. Miken was never late. In all the years he had been going to Desali and doing whatever he did on those islands, he'd never been late. Even when he'd come back early to have Lerato tend to his injuries, Miken had still come back to Alexria on the day he'd promised.

So when the door to her quarters slowly opened and she saw him standing in the doorway, Alexria rushed to him. She wrapped her arms around him in an embrace and buried her face in his neck. Miken held her just as tight.

"I'm back," he kept saying in a whisper. "I'm back."

He smelled like sweat. He felt damp with sweat. In a way, she didn't care. She pulled away from him enough to see his face. He looked at her differently than he had before.

"Are you alright?" she asked.

He'd learned what happened to Allia. The lost answer was now in his eyes. He looked at her as though she were Allia herself. His hesitation, his ache, his fragile emotion. It was all written over his face. And she wanted him to tell her. Not because she needed him to, but so it would lighten him of the weight of the knowledge.

Miken nodded. "I'm alright," he said. "I just missed you, that's all."

* * * * *

Miken dangled his cup in the grip of his fingers and swayed the liquid. The tea had gone cold by now, but watching it sway back and forth in his cup was entrancing. He was the only one left in the Inn's Tavern. When it had emptied out some time ago, Miken assumed it to be late in the night. Alexria had gone to their rented room long before that. Miken had said he'd join her soon, but that was before his mind began wandering. He was haunted by the image of Allia walking next to Duke Sular and his son. Or should he call her Melony instead? Miken closed his eyes. He didn't know what to do anymore. He'd already run through every possible way of explaining the truth to Allia. None of them were good enough. Each explanation was either too ridiculous to be believable or was blunt enough to push her away. And even if Allia did believe him, even if she agreed to leave the only home she could remember and come to Hydia, she couldn't be trusted anymore. She had grown up being told that every Hydian was an enemy and deserved to be treated as such. Allia was a Desalian now. Melony was a Desalian.

Miken set his cup on the table and watched the swirling tea settle. His wrist ached from how long he had been holding it. Allia was gone. Melony was all that was left. So what did that make her?

Footsteps drew Miken's attention and he found Alexria coming to join him in the empty tavern.

"You never came to bed," she said. Her voice was soft as though she had just woken up.

"How late is it?"

"The sky's getting brighter." She slid onto the bench next to him.

Perhaps his headache was more from needing to sleep than from his circling thoughts. Alexria folded her arms on the table and rested her head on her arms. She sighed deeply and closed her eyes. Her hair rested along her back. Her face was peaceful, unlike himself. It soothed him to see that in her. He brushed a strand of hair out of her eyes. She smiled softly. Alexria had changed too in the last eleven years. It wasn't as dramatic as Allia had, but Alexria had certainly grown. She was more of a woman than the girl he had married. She was weathered in a way that made her stronger, more beautiful in a way she couldn't see herself, and matured from seeing more than she should have. He couldn't remember how those changes had happened. He felt as though he should have noticed them before now.

"I don't know where the time went," Miken said.

Her heavy eyes opened to look at him. She had such gentle eyes. He caressed her cheek.

"I can remember everything we used to do," Miken said, "and everything we used to be. But between now and then... I've missed it."

Alexria slid across the bench until he could feel her against him. She kept her head on her arms. Miken settled an arm around her shoulders. Her body felt warm against his own. There was a vague familiarity to it that he hadn't taken the time to feel enough. He used to. There was a lot they used to do that seemed like an old dream now.

"Laren would be fifteen by now," Alexria said, "Allia would be thirteen, and our youngest would be almost eleven."

Thirteen. That may have been her age but Allia - or Melony - had already matured beyond that.

"They'd be old enough to have their own personalities by now," Alexria said as though describing a dream. "They'd have their own childhoods and their own stories. They'd start reminding us of ourselves, too."

Miken could picture that same dream. "We'll never have that, will we?" he said quietly.

Alexria lifted her hand up to where his was on her shoulder. "No we won't."

The acceptance was in her voice. She had accepted that fact for a long time now. She hadn't spent all her years waiting and searching for something she couldn't get back. Miken wanted the peace she had. He needed it. He needed to shut away the thoughts that haunted him.

"We used to dance," Miken said.

Alexria slowly lifted her head at the thought and looked across the room. "Then let's dance," she said, looking back at him.

The tavern was empty and there was an area cleared of tables that was large enough for it, but it was quiet. "There's no music."

"There doesn't have to be."

Alexria took his hand in hers, curling her fingers under his palm. He couldn't remember the last time she held his hand as softly as she did now. It was enough to make him rise up from the bench and lead her to the new dance floor. He lightly touched his free hand to her waist. She touched his shoulder. Their dance began with slow, swaying steps. He watched her feet so he wouldn't step on them. Her boots mirrored his over the wooden floor, following his simple pattern. She moved her hand from his shoulder to the back of his neck. The touch of her skin lifted his gaze to hers, allowing his feet to move on their own. It made her eyes smile.

There was a song they used to dance to. On every good evening whenever Miken was home, they'd go out to the courtyard together. Their servants learned the habit and would already be out there playing a tune. Sometimes they would dance to other songs first and sometimes their children would join them. But they would always end with the same gentle tune. Miken never learned the name of it, but the song and dance were now replaying in his mind.

Miken slowed their dance to a stop and paused for a breath, the way he always use to. Her smile grew to a soft grin. He spun her once then took two quick steps. He smiled back when he felt her keep up with ease. Miken led the rhythm of fast and slow steps. He was guided by the song playing through his mind.

It brought him back to his home. The dirt of their courtyard would dance under their feet. Some evenings the wind would toss around Alexria's hair and she'd let it fly as it pleased. When the wind was calm, each spin would cause her dress to flare. And she was just as beautiful when she danced in her work pants and tunic. They danced as Alexria carried each of their three children and her stomach grew with each passing season. When Laren and then Allia were born, one of the servants would hold them so they could watch from the side. If the dance didn't begin until late, Miken and Alexria would first tuck the children in bed with a story before coming out to the courtyard. They danced through the coloured sky of dusk and the light of lanterns after dark; through calm evenings as well as crisp winds or muggy air or the odd time in the rain. They danced after days when their love was visible to the household and days when their patience was tested. They had danced through life. And for a long time they had forgotten to do that. Until this morning. Until each time Miken spun Alexria away from him, he'd bring her back closer than the time before. Until he at last felt her body against his and felt her soft curves press against his chest. She took one final, slow spin and came back to him again, wrapping her arm around his shoulders. Miken lifted his hand to her cheek and caressed the smooth skin. They couldn't go back to how it had been. He could see in her eyes that she knew that too. He kissed her. It was only light touches to her lips at first and that was enough to make his heart pound. Her embrace clung to him. Her kiss strengthened in a way it hadn't done in years and he returned the passion. He'd missed her. For so long, he'd missed her.

They didn't need to go back. They could go forward.

Chapter 15

Foreign Alliances

After the shipwreck

"**A**lex, at least let me see it," Lerato said as he crouched to be at her level. "Let me see how good or bad it is."

They had been brought to the prison in the bottom of the Petayrn fortress. It was the same prison where the other Hydians were held, which provided some relief in itself. Most of the sailors and Hydian Knights were accounted for, including General Kaytan and the First Mate. Those men that were missing had been killed during the original attack on the ship. Genev was now with her husband and Kaytan was grateful to see her injuries were minimal. Lerato wished the same could be spoken for Alexria. She sat in the back corner of the large room with a hand pressed to her side.

She shook her head. "You don't need to worry about me."

"Whether I see it or not, I'm already worried," Lerato said. "You're my responsibility, remember."

"No, I'm..."

"You are."

Her gaze was down. She didn't have the strength to argue back. She looked tense enough to assume she barely had the strength to maintain her composure.

Lerato eased himself to the stone ground to make the conversation easier. "You're not even supposed to be here," he said. He motioned back to Genev. "You got caught in the middle of our battle."

"If it is meant for our paths to cross then they will," Alexria said. Her voice sounded small. "Lady Samila told me that."

There was a context to it that Lerato didn't understand. That was the way with most of Lady Samila's advice. "What does that mean?"

Alexria lifted her eyes briefly enough to give an answer. "It means I'm meant to be here." She looked down again. "Focus on getting back to Hydia. Don't focus on me."

Lerato didn't want to think she was right. He didn't want to think he was wasting his time helping her. Yet perhaps getting back to Hydia was the only way to help her. What good would it be for him to look at a wound he could do nothing else for?

The bar sealing the prison door could be heard lifting. Lerato rose as the door opened. Whoever the Desalian was would likely be interested in either the Hydian Prince or the General. While most of the sailors remained seated, the Hydians Knights all positioned themselves between the door and where Lerato and Kaytan stood. Kaytan tucked Genev behind himself.

It was Miken that entered, no one else, and the door closed behind him. He stood at the entrance looking over the Hydian crowd.

"Is that...?" Kaytan asked.

"Unfortunately." Lerato hadn't told Kaytan much about what had happened in the banquet hall with the Duke. He didn't know enough about Miken's act to know what to say. Seeing him here only raised more questions and along with them came frustrations. Regardless, Lerato stepped out to the front of the crowd.

"Where's Alex?" Miken asked.

That was the last thing Lerato expected from him. "So, you'll admit you know her now?"

"Where is she?"

"Will you admit you're a Hydian too or is that even true?"

"It's complicated."

There was a cold tone to his composure to suggest he buried the same amount of frustration that Lerato expressed. Lerato wanted that frustration to snap out. He wanted to see the act break and see the true face come out.

"It's always complicated with you."

"I'm not here to fight you," Miken said quietly.

"Then why betray us?" Lerato was tired of carrying unanswered questions. "If you knew this would happen, then why tell Desalians of our plans to set sail? And with Alexria on board?"

"I didn't tell them."

"Then who did?" Lerato wanted to slap some emotion into the man's face. It wouldn't be Prince-like behaviour, but how Prince-like did he need to be while in prison.

"Hydian ships never sail at night," Miken said. "You brought the attention on yourselves."

Lerato fell silent. Miken stated the facts as though they were common knowledge. Perhaps this was a common fact among Desalians. Perhaps Lerato and Kaytan had tried too hard to keep their trip hidden.

Miken closed the distance between himself and Lerato. He focused on Lerato as though the crowd of Hydian Knights and Kaytan didn't exist. "I'm doing all I can to help you."

Lerato lowered his voice. "For Alex, I'll believe that. But there is still one *very* distinct line that needs to be established."

"I'm on Hydia's side."

"Are you?" Lerato asked. "Because in front of the Duke you looked like Desalians owned you."

Miken's pause was only brief. "Where is she?" He spoke as one would ask for permission to see her.

Having already made his point, Lerato stepped aside and motioned for the Hydian Knights to do the same.

"Everyone faces the door," Miken said as he passed by. He held authority as he said it.

If he had that kind of authority, why didn't he force his way past them in the first place? Why did he need their permission to see Alexria?

"Do as he asks," Lerato said loud enough for all the men to hear. He then assured Kaytan's concerned look with, "I'll watch him."

Lerato had seen a lot of Miken over the years and a lot of Alexria, yet it was only now that he realized he had seen little of them together. He had never seen Miken brush the hair from her face as he did now or test the warmth of her skin with the back of his fingers. Lerato was too far away to hear anything more than the murmur of their whispers. Miken sat next to her. He slid one leg between her back and the wall and folded his other leg so he could sit close. Alexria took a red hand away from her side and undid the bandage. Miken took a small jar and cloth from his pocket. He held the cloth over the open lid then, to dampen it, flipped the jar upside-down then right-side-up. Lerato assumed it to be some kind of medicine.

Miken didn't put it on her wound right away. He stroked her hair back again first. He whispered something and she nodded. He offered her his hand and she took it. Then with a slow hand he pressed the cloth against her side. Alexria took a sharp breath. She clenched Miken's hand with one of hers and clenched his leg with the other. She let out a quick breath, allowing a small chirp of pain to escape with it. Her eyes were squeezed closed. She leaned her head back against the wall. With each small, gasping breath the sound of her pain worsened. Lerato felt nauseous.

Alexria began shaking her head. "I can't do it," she said between breaths, "I can't do it."

Miken leaned forward and held a long kiss to her cheek, then leaned his forehead against her temple. He whispered to her. Lerato could only hope the words were encouraging. He turned away from the scene only to find some of the men were glancing back at them.

"Face the door," Lerato said.

Lerato wanted to shut away the sounds. What made it worse was that it was Miken that caused them. It wasn't a Desalian using pain to force information from her; it was Miken trying to tend to the wounds of his wife. When the sounds stopped Lerato hoped to turn to find the scene finished. Instead he saw Alexria slumping over against Miken with the cloth still pressed to her side. She had fainted. It was only then that Lerato went to them. He sat against the wall so Miken's back was to him. Miken cradled Alexria against him like a child.

"Are you alright?" Lerato asked, regretting such an obvious question after he said it. It was a pathetic apology for his recent frustrations.

Miken stroked Alexria's hair instead of answering. "Can your men sail a ship they've never been on before?" he asked. His voice was stale.

Lerato knew little about sailing himself, but the sailors they had brought with them were the best in the Capital. "They could if they had to."

"There's a dock on the east side of this fortress," Miken said. "It comes out at the base of the mountain. That's your way out."

Hearing that helped relax some of Lerato's tension. "When do we leave?"

"You'll need to wait for fog cover, which is often out here. Aside from telling you that, I can't promise how much more help I'll be."

Lerato winced at the last of those words. "That's what I don't understand about you."

"I walk a very fine line."

"Then choose a side," Lerato said. He wished he could see Miken's face more easily. There was little expression on his back.

"As long as I'm the King's Ambassador, they won't question what I do," Miken said, "but as soon as I'm named a Desalian traitor..." His head shook subtly. "... I'll be nothing once that happens."

"I'll finally trust you once that happens."

Miken set aside the now bloody cloth. He untied a knot of cloth under his tunic and unraveled a long strip of cloth from around his waist. He began wrapping the bandage around Alexria's waist.

"I may not trust you," Lerato said, "but I would have taken your place to tend to Alex. You didn't have to be the one to do that."

"You would have stopped part-way," he said quietly. "That would have made it worse for her." He paused for a moment, then added, "I'm not proud to say I could do it."

Alexria's breaths quickened as she stirred. Miken paused his work with the bandage.

"Shh. I'm here," Miken said, stroking her hair. "Just breathe. I'm here."

Alexria relaxed against him. Lerato picked himself up to give them some privacy.

"The last time I fainted was when I saw that thief break his arm," Alex said weakly. Her breaths began to settle.

"This time, I'm glad you did," Miken said.

Lerato stopped at the word 'thief.' When would Alexria have encountered thieves? Lerato remembered Alexria telling him once that they hadn't been to their country home in years. The most news of thieves that Lerato had heard in the last several years has involved news of the new Guardians of Hydia. Between the two of them, they had enough skill.

"You're the new Guardians of Hydia, aren't you?" Lerato asked. He said it quietly. He didn't know why.

It was Alexria that first looked up at him. It wasn't the prideful look that he'd expected if he'd been right, nor was it the confused look from him being wrong. Instead it was most comparable to the guilty look of being caught.

It was Miken that answered. "It's not a title we would have given ourselves," he said.

* * * * *

It was getting better. Alexria's side still ached like nothing else and she still felt uselessly weak, but she wasn't trembling anymore. She wasn't chilled and sweating at the same time. It made the wait easier. Since Miken left their prison cell, Alexria stayed in her seat against the wall. She closed her eyes, hoping she could find some form of rest. She held the vile of strengthening medicine in her hands, waiting for Miken to return so she could drink it. She could hear the other men becoming more restless. The pacing of footsteps, the shifting against stone floors and walls, the whispers, the questions, the sighs. At times listening to it helped keep Alexria away from her own thoughts. But not completely. Her necklace continued to sway into her memory. Each time she tried to form a question, she could barely bring herself past 'How' and 'Why' before she would shy away from asking more. She didn't want to know. She couldn't carry the weight of knowing anymore. She had gotten past it. She had finally gotten past it. But Lady Samila's words hovered in her mind. "*If it is meant for your paths to cross then they will.*" Alexria clung to those words. She repeated them over and over to stop her mind from wandering into any new thoughts of her own. Thoughts such as why she was supposed to be here. What could she possibly do by being here? If her and Allia's paths were meant to cross, why couldn't it have been sooner? Why did Allia's childhood need to be lost? Why hadn't Miken done anything sooner? Why didn't he tell her? Alexria squeezed her eyes closed tighter. Why didn't he tell her?

Alexria heard the clapping of sandals coming toward her. She didn't want to open her eyes. She was too tired to listen to the Princess now.

"Alexria," Princess Genev said gently.

Alexria made herself open her eyes. The Princess stood in front of her, so Alexria needed to tilt her head up to see her. Her arms hugged around her dirt-scuffed cloak. Her hood was down, despite her hair being in a mess. She looked harmless.

"Yes, my lady."

Princess Genev hesitated. She opened her mouth to speak, then paused to adjust her footing, then came to Alexria's side. She sat on the ground beside Alexria, but even that was a series of hesitations and adjustments of her dress. When she made it down, she let out a soft sigh.

"I'm not accustomed to sitting on the ground," Princess Genev said.

"Or crawling through trees," Alexria said.

"No, I suppose not." Her voice was light but quiet. It was comforting to hear for a change.

Alexria leaned her head back against the wall where it was more comfortable.

"Alexria," the Princess said again. She paused before continuing. "I feel I should take blame for your injury."

Alexria shook her head. "You'll learn quick not to play that game with yourself," she said. "If you want to blame someone, then blame the Desalians who did it. But it's not worth taking revenge."

She could feel the Princess looking hard at her. "Have you never wished to take revenge?"

Adicara was the first name Alexria considered. She didn't know how he remembered who she was, but he did. Alexria couldn't remember the last time, or if there was ever a time, when she'd wanted to start a fight with anyone. But in that moment in the forest, when he whispered to her, she did. She could remember wishing her hands hadn't been bound and that her side hadn't been burning. Alexria closed her eyes and breathed away the memory.

"I think everyone's wanted revenge at one time," Alexria said to answer the Princess's question. "Sometimes it's hard not to."

The prison cell door was unbarred and swung open. The attention of every Hydian snapped to it. Alexria drank the vile of medicine in a gulp and then closed her eyes again. It would be Miken returning to say that the fog had settled. He'd then guide them in the escape he'd explained to Lerato and General Kaytan: some of the men would find their way to the moat and swim to the docks while the others fought their way through the fortress to reach the docks in that way. If the timing was right, the group that swam would have the ship ready to sail by the time the second group reached it.

"What did you drink?" Princess Genev asked.

Alexria kept her eyes closed, resting, as she answered. "Medicine to drown the pain."

Alexria would be in the second group, fighting their way through the fortress. Without the medicine, she didn't know how else she'd have the strength to get off the island.

Instead of Miken, a girl's voice spoke in a demanding tone. "The Hydian Prince."

It was the girl they called Melony. The girl Alexria wanted to call Allia but couldn't bring herself to. Melony's sharp gaze found Lerato quickly.

"For what purpose?" General Kaytan asked.

Melony's gaze cut to the General. "The Hydian Prince," she said again.

Lerato walked forward. Melony stepped aside so he could join the guards outside the door and be taken away. Waiting for the fog was taking too long.

"And the maid," Melony demanded.

Alexria felt her chest tighten. As Melony's gaze found her, her throat tightened too. As though a hand had settled around her neck. They were Allia's eyes. Allia's sweet little eyes all grown up and holding the shadow of all the darkness she's seen in Desali.

"Bring her forward," Melony said.

It was General Kaytan that came to help her up. She needed it. Her legs were stiff and her side continued to ache and complain at her.

"Are you any better?" the General asked in a whisper.

Alexria gestured she was with a few short nods. "I can walk on my own," she said quietly. "Thank-you." She gave him a weak smile which he tried to return.

Alexria walked to her. She hoped her steps were not as slow as they felt. Fifteen years ago Allia hadn't been able to walk yet. She could crawl. She'd gained the strength to crawl quickly. Now Melony was standing before Alexria with a hand on the hilt of her sword, their eye-line nearing the same level. Her face was like stone. Her eyes were cold. What had happened?

"The necklace," Melony said. "I want to know your story."

The story of the necklace. Had anyone else asked her she may not have answered. There were too many people here. But this was Allia's story. It was Melony's story. But did she call Melony her daughter? Did she call Miken her husband?

As Alexria began, she couldn't hold her gaze with Melony's. "I've had the necklace since I was a girl. When... when my daughter was born, my husband had the same one made for her." She had wanted to say 'When you were born,' but she couldn't bring herself to say it. She reached for the necklace she wore. "This is hers. She was holding mine on the day she was taken from me. That was fifteen years ago."

Melony's face was like stone. No expression, no emotion, no consideration of thought. She looked the way Miken did when he refused to reveal too much of himself to someone he didn't trust. Melony turned to leave. How could she leave? How could she not want to know more? There had to be some part of her that was curious and that longed to keep searching. There was so much more she needed to know.

"Melony," Alexria called after her.

The girl kept walking.

"Melony, wait."

The thud of the closing door echoed through the room.

* * * * *

The young Desalian commander, Sinele, if Lerato remembered his name correctly, was waiting in the cell Lerato was brought to.

Sinele leaned against the wall polishing a dagger with a cloth. The boy was too young to have that much confidence. Miken had been right about him and his reckless nature.

"Tie him up," Sinele said.

If Lerato's sense of direction was accurate, the prison cell he was led into would be relatively above the cell of the other Hydians. However they had woven through several passages, including one with a staircase, to reach this room. Inside there were two thick wooden poles reaching from floor to ceiling. Lerato's arms were stretched between the two of them and chained there. His shoulders tensed. It was a very different feeling to be standing here in this way. He had seen it done to various prisoners over the years, but had never experienced the vulnerability of it until now. There was little movement that the chains allowed of his arms. He'd barely be able to turn or back away from anything coming toward him. The tense frustration of his shoulders spread toward his chest. He was useless to whatever reckless intentions Sinele had.

"I'm not as patient as my father," Sinele's voice came from behind him. "He'll negotiate and talk until he can reach some 'bargain that is best for both parties' because he's too afraid to kill you."

"He's wise."

"He's soft," Sinele snapped back. "Every day you Hydians are left untouched is a day we have surrendered to the fear of Hydia's power."

Lerato couldn't help but laugh at the boy's words. "And who convinced you of that?"

The edge of Sinele's dagger pressed against Lerato's side. "Every Desalian knows it."

"Except your father."

Sinele hit him hard in the side and Lerato keeled over as much as he could at the unexpected blow. He coughed to get his breath back.

"Reasonable negotiations will end this war before more death will," Lerato said with frustration seeping through his voice.

Sinele finally walked into Lerato's view. "And what 'reasonable negotiation' are you willing to offer?"

"Peaceful waters and trade would be a decent start." But as Lerato said it he remembered the wall he was talking to.

Sinele smiled and shook his head. "You live on land *we* deserve and you offer us trade?" He took a long contemplative breath. He looked like a boy. "This guard here," he said, motioning behind Lerato, "is going to introduce you to his whip. Now unless you or your Hydians listening below you provide a more 'reasonable' bargain, I doubt you'll be able to interrupt him." He stepped closer to Lerato, his dagger hanging impatiently in his hand. The dagger raised to the skin of Lerato's wrist as Sinele spoke. "And I'd suggest you think quickly, because you're running out of time."

Lerato didn't flinch as the blade sliced the skin. His wrist burned with new pain as Sinele grinned and left the room. He could feel the heat of blood swelling to the cut. The first strike of a whip struck Lerato's back and he groaned at it, more in anger than pain. 'Reckless' now seemed more than appropriate.

Chapter 16

The Last to Fall

2 years before the shipwreck

Miken walked the rocky Hydian shore before returning to Alexria. It was still early enough for her to be asleep and he found the walk was helpful in clearing his mind of everything he'd just seen in Desali. The political meetings, rumours of plots, conflicts of strategies, and childlike bickering all faded away with each step. Here the cool breeze was refreshing instead of chilling. He couldn't explain why.

He stopped once he was far enough away from docks of the Capital and turned to face the water. The sky was coloured with deep ribbons of orange from the morning. The sun itself was still beneath the line of the water. He breathed in the salty air. He'd much rather be here, in Hydia, chasing down thieves and raising barns. It was more... rewarding, more satisfying. It was more of a life than anything Desali could offer. Miken sat down on a flat rock facing the ocean. He and Alexria had a life again. The thought made him smile.

When he heard footsteps coming from further down the shore, Miken wasn't surprised. Every time Miken came here in the mornings, the same man with a fishing pole and bucket would be on his way back home. Miken had begun greeting him as a familiar face. The name wasn't important.

This time the fisherman had someone else walking with him. The play of morning light and shadow made it difficult to see who the visitor was at a distance. The fisherman raised his arm as a casual wave and Miken did the same. The visitor carried no fishing pole or bucket of his own. The two of them were merely walking and talking. As they came closer Miken noted that the visitor was an older man. There was a subtle limp in one of his legs, but he still carried some of the strength from his youth. There was a familiar nature about him that Miken couldn't shake.

"Mornin', sir. It's good to see you again," the fisherman said as they approached.

"Likewise," Miken said.

"This is Ari," the fisherman said. "A good friend of mine."

Ari, or Arimon as he was also called, was a man Miken met years ago. It was Arimon who first convinced Miken that turning against Desali was possible. He'd said that Miken wasn't bound to the Desalian life he was born into. Unless things had changed since they last spoke, Arimon was a slave in the neighbouring kingdom of Rylan, west of Hydia. But a long time ago, before Miken was old enough to remember, Arimon had been one of the Old Guardians of Hydia.

"Do you mind if I visit here a little longer?" Arimon asked the fisherman.

"Take all the time you need," the fisherman said with a nod and a smile. "She's a good mornin' for it." He then carried on over the rocks, leaving the Arimon and Miken time on their own.

For a long moment Arimon watched the fisherman leave before sitting next to Miken on the rocks. He still had the stature of the swordsman and archer that the stories described him as. The question was more of whether he still carried the skill behind the stature. He certainly didn't carry the lifestyle anymore. How could that be possible of a slave? Even the stories say that of the Old Guardians of Hydia, Arimon was the last to fall. To the people, he didn't exist anymore.

"I thought you avoided Hydia," Miken said.

"One of my masters is visiting the Hydian Capital," Arimon said. "I'm only a face in the crowd now." He didn't seem to take any offense by the comment. Miken hadn't meant any by it.

They were quiet for a long moment, looking out at the water and the rolling waves on the shore. A patch of the sky was beginning to glow brighter from the approaching sunrise.

"I've heard rumours of new Guardians of Hydia," Arimon said.

Miken had also heard the title. It was a dangerous thing to be called and wasn't something he ever planned on using to refer to himself. "They're only rumours," Miken said, brushing it off.

Arimon glanced at him. "The first time we heard that title used for us, it was more of an intimidation than an honour. I can remember thinking to myself that the title itself was more likely to get us killed than anything else."

"It did." The stories never described it as that, but Miken knew enough of Desali to assume that the Guardians of Hydia had been hunted men in those days.

Arimon leaned his arms on his knees. "A 'King' may be killed for his title. Same with a 'Prince' or a 'Duke.' Even the title of 'Hydian' can be dangerous to have in some parts. Yet a 'Guardian of Hydia' is not so much killed for their title as it is their actions."

"Encouraging," Miken said in a sarcastic tone. "Is that why you're hiding in Rylan?"

Arimon gave a patient smile. "I have a purpose to fill in Rylan."

"Such as?"

"I don't know," Arimon said after a pause. "The Greater Power hasn't revealed that yet."

Miken had heard the Greater Power mentioned from time to time. Though usually he heard it from a Desalian and usually it was referred to as Hydia's crutch.

"You don't believe He exists, do you?" Arimon asked. He said it as though he had already considered the answer to his honest question.

Miken made a light shrug. "I'd rather make my own choice than wait for an answer that wasn't guaranteed to come."

Arimon nodded understandably. "You should, though."

"I should do a lot of things."

"Miken." Arimon sounded like a father when he called his attention like that.

After a pause, Miken looked at him to hear whatever speech he had for him.

"You've already spent time speaking with Him," Arimon said. "The least you can do is believe He exists."

Miken made an amused smiled. He wasn't sure why he did. Perhaps it was the easiest thing to do. "When have I ever talked to the Greater Power?"

Arimon nodded toward the Hydian docks. "Just this morning is one example."

Miken's smile faded. This morning? Miken slowly looked in the direction of the docks. The only person between here and there, still making his way over the sunlit rocks, was the fisherman. Miken raked a slow hand through his hair. The sun had risen enough to cast the man in light, but he was still just a fisherman.

"The Greater Power is a man?"

Arimon folded his hands patiently. "Would you have listened to a strange voice you heard on the wind?" he asked. "Or to... a wolf if it started speaking to you?"

Miken knew the answer was 'no' to both questions, but it seemed Arimon didn't need him to say it.

"Or would you have trusted an armed General if he came to you on horseback?" Arimon asked.

"I wouldn't trust any armed stranger," Miken said.

The creases in Arimon's face smiled. "But the familiar face of a common fisherman is someone you'd listen to. So that is what He became for you."

Miken looked back to the fisherman. He was in the distance near the docks. The first time he'd met the fisherman had been the first day he'd searched for Allia in Desali. Miken had been sitting on these rocks, spinning his dagger, and losing himself in thought. The relief that dagger could have given him had been tempting.

"I think he saved my life," Miken said, speaking his thought.

"He has a purpose for you as a Guardian of Hydia," Arimon said. "You'll find you won't always know exactly what your purpose is, just as I don't know the rest of mine. You only need to remember that you have one."

Miken didn't know what to say to that. He couldn't counter it. He didn't know how.

"I didn't come to discuss what you should or should not be called," Arimon said. "Being a Guardian of Hydia, like any true servant, is not a title you choose. It is a life you choose. I came here this morning to thank you."

They had chosen that life, hadn't they. Miken couldn't quite explain how it happened. It began as an escape from an empty space they each had in them, it became something that somehow filled that space, and now it was who they were. Whether they wanted that title or not, whether it put them in danger's way or not, it was who they were.

"It won't be an easy life," Arimon said, "but you won't be alone in it."

"But is it a life worth dying for?" Miken asked.

Arimon had patient eyes. His age only seemed to add that to them. "My brother, Alecan, who was another Old Guardian of Hydia, told me it was. I believe it will be. Yet I suppose it's not something you'll know completely until your final moments."

Chapter 17

Raising Swords

After the shipwreck

For a long moment, Alexria stood staring at the door. Melony was gone. Alexria had lost the one chance she had to convince her of the truth. Instead the cell door remained closed and there were no hopeful sounds of it opening soon. They would have to open it themselves. They couldn't keep sitting here waiting for their sentence. If Alexria was to be any help, they'd need to leave soon. For now the medicine was working quickly, but she didn't know how long it would last. The ache in her side was numbing and the heavy fatigue of her body was fading away.

The Hydians around her were also becoming restless. Some of the Hydian Knights spoke with General Kaytan in hushed, frustrated voices. Alexria wanted to join, wanted to know what was being planned. But she had barely ever spoken with the General. If Lerato had been among them, she wouldn't have hesitated as much to interrupt.

The cell door opened, stealing the attention of everyone inside. But no one acted on it. If they were to get out, they'd have to fight their way out of an already open door.

A young man, or rather a boy, entered with six Desalian Guards. He was the Duke's son. The name 'Sinele' felt familiar. The

Desalian Guards spread out so they stood between the Hydians and Sinele and Sinele didn't waste any time waiting for them to get in position.

"Now if you listen carefully," Sinele said to the room, "you'll hear the beating that your Prince is currently receiving."

In his pause, Alexria heard the faint echo of a whip in the halls.

Sinele went on. "Your Prince has refused to make a reasonable offer. So unless his people speak for him, his life will quickly run short."

"An offer for what?" the General asked. Of the Hydians in the room, he and Princess Genev had the most authority. But the Princess was less likely to speak with that authority.

"Offer something I want and I will give you the freedom you want," Sinele said it as if it were an obvious answer.

Sinele had left the cell door open. There were only six Guards in the room compared to nearly thirty Hydians. The Hydians were unarmed and half were sailors instead of Knights, but they had the numbers.

"The only offer you'd except would mean the death of Hydia," the General said.

Sinele's face grew hard. "Well, then, if your lives mean nothing to you, I'll have to take them one at a time until you reconsider." His eyes were floating over the crowd, searching for a target. He stopped when he saw Alexria. "Kill the maid."

The Guard closest to Alexria came at her with his dagger. Her heart started to beat faster.

"She's already injured," the General said in objection.

"A small loss then."

To Sinele she'd be the weakest in the room, not as valuable as the Princess, but innocent enough to pull at the hearts of the men. The Guard coming at her seemed to think the same. He approached the way he may approach a defenceless child. Someone who wouldn't resist because of fear. But when the Guard was within a step of

Alexria, with his dagger low, she sent a high punch to his cheek. The Guard was knocked back, not expecting the strike. Alexria took the hand holding the dagger and twisted it until it crippled him. A Hydian Knight near her swung his fist hard into the Guard's stomach. The Guard's hand loosened enough for her to take the dagger and she swung the hilt down to the back of his head. The Guard fell still to the ground.

That was all the Hydians needed. One person to act. Before Alexria had finished knocking down the one Guard, the Hydians had turned against the other Guards in the room. Sinele paled and dashed for the door. Alexria caught him and wrapped an arm around his neck in the way Miken had shown her before. She locked her grip tight. Sinele grabbed at her arm and reached back for her face. Alexria closed her eyes. Her side still had a faint ache to it. Sinele faded quickly, dropping to his knees and then becoming limp. Alexria held her grip for a moment longer to be safe.

All six Desalian Guards now lay still on the ground and three Hydian men had been badly injured in the process. Two more guards raced in from the hallway and were knocked down quickly.

The Hydian Knights, now armed with weapons they'd gathered, charged into the prison hallway and divided themselves to the left and right. Though Alexria followed them out, it took only moments before the scuffle was over and the remaining Desalians lay either dead or unconscious. The Knights gathered up any weapons they could find while General Kaytan stood in the cell doorway to keep the other Hydians from flooding out. He was stern with thought.

"Alexria," the General said, calling her to him.

"Sir?"

"Lerato told me your title," he said.

That took all words from her completely. Carrying the title of Guardians of Hydia was safest when it wasn't widely known. And spreading news of that title here, in Desalian territory, was likely the most dangerous place to be.

"I want you to join the group splitting away to find Lerato," he said. "You'll be useful to them."

He spoke with the commanding tone of giving an order. Alexria wasn't used to hearing it or being told what to do in that way. But she nodded and breathed. Her wound was becoming more manageable. It only needed to last until they reached the docks.

And as for Allia... or Melony... Alexria didn't know what to do yet. When Miken had come to this cell to tend to Alexria's side, one of the first things she said was, "She's here."

Miken had stroked the sweaty hair away from her face. "I know. Let's get you out first, alright," he had said. "I need to get you out first."

* * * * *

Despite how small the island of Petayrn was, there were three docks on its shoreline. It was, of course, home to more sailors than any other Desalian island and the ships tied to the docks were only a fragment of the Petayrn-owned vessels roaming the seas. The dock at the base of the fortress was more of an open mouth to a cave and was mostly for private use of the Duke and his military. Miken had noticed the pattern of this dock early in his visits. As long as the weather permitted, a single ship could always be found tied here with enough sailors ready to man it. The only exceptions were when heavy storms rose up or during dawn or dusk when the ship would sail on to its next destination and another would be expected to soon take its place. Miken wasn't surprised when he came down the passage of stone steps to see the same ship he had arrived on this morning.

"Short visit again, Sir?" the Desalian Captain called as Miken climbed from the small rowboat up to the ship.

"Are you still headed toward Deslalda?" Miken pulled out a leather pouch of coins already counted.

"We are. We'll arrive at Emyl first before circling back to it."

Miken tossed the pouch to the Desalian Captain who then weighed it in his hand and said, "I'll assume you're on board when we leave, then."

Miken nodded. "That's always appreciated." Miken's travelling habits were known by most Desalian Captains by now. He'd pay for passage regardless of whether he planned to travel or not. Sometimes he'd make it clear when he was boarding, sometimes he'd board more subtly, and other times he'd board like a stowaway. It made his path harder to trace and his plans harder to predict. On the islands, it was a form of survival.

"What are your thoughts on the weather?" Miken asked.

"The skies 'll be clear," the Desalian Captain said, looking up and out over the water. "But the sea 'll do as she wants. Like you do."

As Miken surveyed the water, he caught a glimpse of someone swimming near the mouth of the fortress moat. He almost forgot to grin at the man's comment. He looked away from the swimmer so as not to draw attention to it yet. It was too soon for the swimmer to be one of the Hydian prisoners. But he needed to kill time before he could steal another look.

"It's nothing you can't tame, from what I hear," Miken said.

"The sea or you, Sir?"

Miken raised his eyebrows to caution his humour.

The Desalian Captain cleared his throat and continued. "There hasn't been a storm in all my years that's kept me off the water. Now you won't hear that from no Hydian sailor."

"Hydians have nowhere to go," Miken said with a scoff.

"Exactly." The man leaned back against the rail of the ship. "Hydian sailors can afford to be weak. I tell you if Hydia's Capital were on their island, we'd have taken it long ago."

The man waved his hands to paint the picture he imagined, giving Miken another chance to look out at the water. He could only see where the mouth of the moat opened up to drink from the salt water of the ocean. A wall of rock rose up on each side, one side being the rock of the island and other behind the mountain base of the fortress. The swimmer was against the rock of the fortress. He also noticed three figures instead of only the one. And there were likely more hiding out of his view. The Hydians had made their escape much sooner than they should have. There was no fog to cover them and no shadow of night to hide them. Miken wanted to wave to them to go back but it would be too late. Another Hydian group would already be on their way through the fortress. He'd have to help them from here as best he could. And, for now, that meant distracting the Desalian Captain from the water and waiting for the best moment to take action.

"Do you think a shoreline battle could be won from the sea?" Miken asked. He began strolling toward the cabins and the Desalian Captain followed.

Capturing and binding the men on board wasn't an option this time since they would have witnessed Miken helping the Hydians escape. Witnesses like that were too dangerous for him. He'd need to kill them instead.

"Are you planning to take the Capital, Sir?"

The eagerness of the man's voice took away Miken's sympathy. "I'm here for your thoughts not my plans," Miken said coldly.

The man cleared his throat. "With the Capital's fortress being nearly a thousand strides from the docks, the only shoreline battle there'd be is to unload men. Unless the battle's brought to us, I'll be no more useful than a cargo ship."

They reached the cabin belonging to the Desalian Captain and Miken closed the door behind them. "How do we bring the fight to us?"

"Sir?"

"You can't say you haven't thought of it," Miken said, coaxing the man's pride. "Every Desalian can say how their sword will be the one to bend Hydia to its knees. Unless you're a 'humble Hydian.'"

The man grinned in amusement as he lowered himself into his wide chair. Miken found a chair of his own.

"How will your ship bend Hydia?" Miken asked.

How long would it take the Hydians to swim to the ship? No shouts of alarm had been heard yet. If Miken waited until the first shouts of warning, he'd be able to move his sword through the ship without hesitation. If he moved earlier he'd have to act so as not to sound any alarms himself.

"A battle at sea would leave the Hydians spinning as we manoeuvred and boarded them," the Desalian Captain said. "It would be over only moments after it began."

"How would you get them to sea?"

The Desalian Captain made a large shrug with his arms. "Drop their princess on a rock and tell them to fetch. They value pathetic lives enough that they'll flock like birds to a fresh catch."

Miken didn't make the effort to force an approving smile. "And if that doesn't work?"

"Then we flood the Capital," the man said. "We'll empty their Capital of its people until they open the fortress gates. I'd wager it'd take no more than a day before they break. We'd also have less Hydians to deal with after that day."

Too many Desalians thought as this man did. Too many were willing to kill who they had to to get what they wanted. Whether they killed Hydians or Desalians, Kings or peasants, men or children, it didn't matter. That was who these men were. It was who they were raised to be. There was no sense trying to change them. How could he change men who would claim another man's child as his own? Too many times Miken had sat to the side and watched it all happen. He'd been bound to his title of Ambassador. He had feared the response of the King, or his brother if he could bring himself to call Mehera that. What kind of people lived in fear of their own brothers?

"Well," Miken said to the Desalian Captain as he stood, "I suppose it's good we don't value pathetic lives."

Miken drew a dagger and threw it in a single motion. The blade buried into the Desalian Captain's chest and his eyes were wide as Miken snapped his neck to the side. The Hydians swimming here should be close enough by now. Miken pulled out his dagger and cleaned it on the dead man's shirt. He'd never killed in cold blood within Desali territory before. He'd considered it and wanted to. Part of him wanted this news to spread to the King, so his rebellion wasn't a secret anymore. But he could never justify the risk. Not if it risked Alexria too. No, word of this couldn't spread. Any man who saw his face couldn't live to tell of it.

The Desalian flag hung in the cabin. The three waves of colour taunted him; a deep blue wave in the middle, red above it, black beneath it. Miken cut off a black strip and tied it around his mouth and nose. It would be easier to kill without worrying about survivors.

* * * * *

The snapping sound of the whip guided Alexria and the group of Hydian Knights. The slow rhythm echoed and bounced through the passages. Alexria tried not to count but she also didn't need to for her to know the number was getting high. The Knights that came with her, the General's four most trusted men, were rushing more than she wanted to. Each time they turned a corner they met at least one Desalian guard, sometimes a handful. They were easy kills and an easy collection of weapons, but they were testing chance. And every time she saw a man laying on the ground with a fatal wound, she couldn't help but wonder if that death had been avoidable. It wasn't until they found a curling staircase that they found their match. They climbed up one level toward the sound only to meet a long hallway of armed Desalian men. Lerato was at the far end.

The first Knight to reach the hallway shouted back over his shoulder to the others. "Keep moving."

The hallway was a blur after that. Alexria followed the charge of the Knights with swords swinging. She didn't know when the snapping of the whip stopped. Some swings of their swords struck metal, some struck flesh. They plowed their way through with a charging run until they reached Lerato's open cell at the far end, where the hallway split to the left and the right. Alexria and the four Knights divided themselves among the three directions, two men faced the main hall, one man turned to the left, and Alexria turned to the right with the fourth Knight. The passage was barely wide enough for the two of them, but it slowed the swarm of Desalians charging forward. They would have been surrounded by them otherwise. Alexria focused on them one at a time. She swept her sword back and forth. She forced aside any oncoming, threatening metal and struck at flesh in whatever way she could. An elbow to the nose, a hilt to the back of the head, the strike of a fist, the thrust of a knee, or, if she had to, the slash of her sword. She struck down several men before one of their fists knocked her off her feet. She fell hard on the flat of her back. It stunned her, knocked the wind out of her. She rolled to one side as a sword plunged down. She kicked him as hard as she could manage. Then the sword of the Knight next to her drove into the Desalian's stomach. Alexria climbed back to her feet. It was only as she did that she noticed the silence. For the moment, their path was free of opponents.

Alexria joined the two Knights that went into Lerato's cell. Lerato stood facing away from them with his arms chained to two poles. His back was a web of red lashes from the whip. His head drooped, his legs were weak, and it seemed his arms were supporting most of his weight. One of the Knights reached him before she did.

"My wrist," he said in a tired voice.

When the Knight noticed it he took a tight grip of Lerato's wrist and asked the other Knight for some cloth. There was blood all down Lerato's sleeve and some of his side. Alexria noticed keys hanging on the wall near the door. She brought them to Lerato and began unlocking his shackles as the Knights bandaged his wrist. His face was pale. Even his shackles had pained him, leaving a red band on his skin where the metal had been. Alexria wished she had spare medicine to offer him. She didn't feel she needed as much as she'd taken.

The first Knight helped support Lerato's weight. "Can you walk, Sir?" he asked.

"I'll run if I have to," Lerato said. There wasn't as much strength in his voice as he may have hoped. "Which way to get out of here?"

One of the Knights outside the cell let out a groan and clenched his thigh where an arrow had pierced it. Another Knight pulled him into the shelter of the crossing hallway. The archer stood in the main hall with a clear shot into the cell. Lerato was pulled to the side by the Knights with him. Alexria was about to follow until she looked at the archer. There was only one.

"Melony!"

Melony didn't release the second arrow. It was ready to. She stood at the end of the hall with the arrow sitting on her bowstring and pulled back.

"Get out of the hallway," one of the Knights hissed.

Alexria held up a hand to keep them from acting. She didn't risk taking her eyes off Melony, as though breaking that gaze would be to break everything she had left of the girl.

"Melony," Alexria said more cautiously.

"Alex, we don't have time for this," Lerato said.

"Then leave ahead of me," Alexria said. "I'll catch up."

An arrow flew through the cell door and cut the air between Alexria and where Lerato stood out of Melony's view. Alexria stiffened.

"No one's leaving," Melony said.

"Alright," Alexria said. She sheathed her sword, whether it was wise or not, and began stepping forward. "I just want to talk to you."

"You don't even know me."

Alexria wished she did. She wished so much that she did. "You're right. You're right, I don't."

"And I should kill you where you are."

The fact that she hadn't released this arrow yet was kept Alexria walking. "Come with us."

This was the only answer Melony hesitated with. "You don't know what that means."

That was better than a rejection. "I do know," Alexria said gently. "I know what it's like to leave everything behind. To not know if you'll be coming back to it. I've made that decision before."

Melony said nothing. From a distance, Melony's ready arrow looked steady and controlled. But as Alexria neared it, she noticed there was a slight tremble to it.

"But you're right, I don't know your life," Alexria said. "I wish I did but I don't. I don't know if your life here is worth leaving. I don't know if you can do better than this. Only you do." She hesitated before saying the words she knew she had to say. "And if this life is good I don't want to take that from you."

Alexria was only a stride from Melony now. The arrow remained mostly steady despite the heavy breaths that Melony had built up. Her eyebrows twitched the way Miken's could. She was so much like him. In more ways that maybe Miken would want to admit.

The sound of approaching footsteps came from behind Melony, in the passage of the staircase. Alexria and Melony held their gaze.

"Come with us," Alexria said in a near whisper.

If Melony couldn't release the arrow herself, would she let other Desalians make the killing strike for her? Is that the result that Alexria was standing here waiting for? And if not, if Melony let Alexria live, what would be the fate of the Desalians? The heavy steps continued closer. Soon three armed Desalians appeared in the stairway and rushed toward them. Alexria could feel her heart begin to pound faster. She couldn't draw her sword. Or even raise her fist. If this was to be the death of one of them, she'd rather it be her own than her daughter's.

Melony turned the arrow on her own men and released it toward one. She then drew a second arrow and then a third, using them to strike down the other two men. The steps of Lerato and the other Hydians could be heard behind Alexria. Their escape path was clear again.

"If I go with you," Melony said without turning, "I'll be marked for dead in Desali."

"We'll protect you."

"That's not possible."

Alexria could only think of Miken. The only reason he wasn't marked for dead was because of the fine line he walked to maintain their trust. That was what Alexria understood of it. "Let us try."

Melony stood for a moment with her head partly turned as though listening to, or evaluating, the approaching Hydians. With a shrug of her shoulder she took off the quiver she carried and held her bow out to the side for it to be taken from her. She looked like a surrendering captive.

"I doubt you could," she said quietly.

Lerato and the others reached them. "Alex?" he asked, sounding out of breath.

Alexria took the bow and the quiver. "We've gained a friend," she said.

Melony's lowered eyes looked back as though the words surprised her. Alexria offered a soft smile. It was a start. Just as knocking on the door to their old home was a start to finally returning there.

Chapter 18

Lost Roads

2 years before the shipwreck

Alexria and Miken were on the Western edge of Hydia, somewhere near the North Dividing River. That was all they knew. Losing their bearings was rare for them. This was especially true for Miken more than Alexria herself. Between the strength of the storm and the struggle with their horses, they had lost track of their direction. The forest they walked their horses through offered no shelter. The wind and rain tore through the branches of even the more sturdy trees. They were sure they were now headed in the direction of the river. Once they found the river they would have a sure guide to lead them to the nearest village. But the river was taking too long to reach. Miken wouldn't show his worry any more than she would, whether it was present or not. Alexria could barely feel her fingers anymore. The reigns were becoming harder to hold and her horse continued to argue against her guidance.

The forest cleared into what seemed to be a road, which was a mess of mud and puddles, beside a field. They shouldn't have met a road before reaching the river. They looked to the left and right several times. It made sense to follow the road, but going the wrong way was the difference between a roof to sleep under and a long night of wandering.

"I think I see a light," Miken said. He was looking to the left.

Alexria strained her eyes. The storm blurred everything. The wind blew rain into her eyes. There was nothing but grey and darkness. Then there was something. The faintest of lights. Alexria couldn't be sure if it was really a light or if it was her eyes fooling her. Miken seemed willing enough to try that direction. So was she. If it became nothing they could always turn around.

Yet as they went the light remained steady. Alexria kept her eyes on it, afraid to look away and lose sight of the blurred dot. Miken's pace had quickened. Hopeful. The light became part of a larger shadow, like the outline of a building. The light itself became a certainty. Their boots sloshed through the mud. The shelter was close. A warm fire and dry clothes were close.

Miken stopped. He stopped so suddenly that Alexria went a few steps past him before she realized it.

"What is it?"

Miken was staring at the shelter ahead. "We're home."

Alexria felt as though her heart stopped. The shadow of the shelter had taken shape now. It was a tall and straight wall with a couple peeks of the houses inside. The light was a lantern hanging on the top right corner of the high door. And to the side of the wall and still a vague shadow was their barn. Their home was, had been, near the Western border of Hydia. Near the river. Thirteen long years ago.

"We need to go in," Miken said.

Alexria was shivering from the cold. Her body longed to be dry. Her legs longed to rest. But not there. Out here there was only a storm. In there were memories.

Miken took her hand. She barely felt the cold touch.

"It's time, Alex."

Alexria couldn't bring herself to move. "I'm not ready."

Miken looked at their home and then back at her. "I don't think we'll ever be."

He waited for her. Waited for her to make the first steps that she couldn't find the courage to take.

"Alex."

She looked at him. His hair was a wet mop on his head. His cloths clung to him. His face had little rivers streaming down it. His eyes... Despite the storm, his eyes were warm and inviting. The way she wanted their home to be. The way their home used to be.

"We need to go in," he said again.

Alexria took the first step. Then the second. Then she was walking. Walking up the old road she had spent so many years avoiding. Walking to the place she had spent so long forgetting. The storm made the home look like a dream. Like it would be swept away in the wind the way a cloud would. Yet the closer she got to it the more definite the lines became. Until she was standing at the front gate. Standing in the light of the lantern. It was the same lantern. Miken raised his hand, hesitated, then banged against the wooden door to wake someone inside.

"It may not be ours anymore," Alexria said. She didn't know why she said it. Or where the thought had come from. A fear maybe. An excuse to turn around again.

Miken looked at her thoughtfully. "Maybe," he said. "But they wouldn't turn us away in the storm." He banged on the door again. Then a third time.

Just as Alexria began to wonder if the place had been abandoned, the door opened. A light appeared from inside and a man came out holding another lantern. It was Nevik. The same servant they had had all those years ago, only an older man.

Nevik looked at who they were and then smiled. "It's good to have you home."

Chapter 19

Guarding Sails

After the shipwreck

Miken secured his mask in a tight knot behind his neck. A frantic pounding bombarded the Desalian Captain's door along with shouts from a Desalian man outside. The Hydians had been spotted. Miken drew a second dagger before throwing the door open and killing the sailor quickly. He didn't look at the man's face. He didn't slow his stride once he started out the door. Instead of heading directly out to the main deck, Miken went to the lower levels of the ship where Desalians were scrambling to gather weapons to react to the shouts of alarm. The death count rose as quick as Miken's daggers would move. Five. Seven. Twelve. Miken left them where they fell. He tried to ignore how easy of a kill sailors were compared to trained guards.

He reached the deck to find it empty. The sounds of battle were taking place on the stone slab of the deck and the Hydians swinging the swords were all dry. The swimmers were still in the water making a dash toward the ship. Miken threw three ropes down toward them for when they arrived.

The battle on the deck appeared to be a hopeful struggle. More of the fallen men were Desalian than Hydian. Princess Genev was safely huddled in the entrance of the tunnel and guarded by Hydian swords. Alexria would likely be with her. The overhanging roof of the cave protected the deck from any arrows from the fortress above them. But as soon as they tried to ready the ship and as soon as they ventured out from under the cave's protection to set sail, arrows would rain like a thick mist. They should have waited for the cover of fog.

Miken rowed from the ship to the docks, traded his daggers for a sword, and strode into the heart of the battle. He kept his pace steady and his sword swinging against Desalians until he reached the wide tunnel on the other side. Genev was there with four Hydian guards, but not Alexria. She wasn't out fighting on the dock either.

Miken tugged his mask off his face so Genev would at least recognize him. "Where's Alex?"

Her eyes squinted. "You?" she said in a breath. "She's finding Lerato."

"Where?"

"He was taken from our cell."

Miken turned and started up the gradual stairs of the passage. He pulled his mask back up over his mouth and nose.

"We need you here," Genev called after him.

Miken's jog became a run. Lerato could have been taken to either another corner of the prison or to the banquet hall to speak to the Duke again. The reasons why was another matter that there wasn't time to consider. He'd deal with that when he found them. But what direction was he to go in?

Before Miken had a chance to decide a direction, the hallway began humming with the sound of running feet and shaking armor. Their Desalian boots were the first thing to come into view. They ran three abreast down the steps of the passage and Miken counted at least six rows. They all blurred together after a point. Shouts of warning were sent from the first row to the last and swords were drawn. There were enough men to overwhelm the unsuspecting Hydians on the dock. But here, with the Desalians forced to approach no more than three at a time and Miken's blades already hot with blood, it was more of a challenge than a threat. And fighting guards was more justifiable than fighting sailors. It was more honourable and satisfying. Miken checked his mask was tight, and then began.

* * * * *

There was a fight in the passages of Petayrn's fortress. Alexria and her group were close to the docks. The low end of the stairs glowed in daylight instead of the fire from torches. Whoever was fighting this crowd of Desalians was blocking them from reaching the docks themselves. Alexria and three Hydians Knights came upon the Desalians from behind, taking them by surprise. Lerato, Melony, and the injured Knight stood watching a few steps behind. The crowd of Desalians thinned quickly from there. There was only one man fighting the crowd from the other side. A masked man with Miken's efficient strokes and movements. His sword slashed and sliced and thrust at whatever vulnerable flesh it could find. With every body that fell he found another to take its place. He never paused. His hair was laced with sweat. There was a small, red rip on his shoulder and his hip. And his eyes... His eyes flamed in a way she had never seen before. His eyes shared the same dark passion that drove his sword and littered the passage with dead men. After all the Desalians had fallen, and Miken removed his mask, Alexria almost hoped it was someone else instead.

"Miken?" Lerato said in surprise.

Miken's eyes were skimming over the fallen men, searching for movement. "Go to the ship and get it moving," he said. "I'll clear out the archers for you."

The three armed Knights stood ahead of them in the passage, ready to continue. Lerato, Melony, and the injured Knight started toward them.

"Mike-" Alexria started.

"Go. Don't wait for me."

One of the fallen Desalians started coughing and gasping. Alexria closed her eyes at the sound that came from a few steps behind her. Desalian or not, her heart went to the man. Miken's eyes cut toward the sound and started toward it. Alexria sheathed her sword and moved into Miken's path. When he stepped around her, she stepped into his way again and put her hands on his arms. She had to take a step backwards before he stopped.

"At least spare one man," she said in a whisper. It probably wouldn't make a difference. The man would probably die on his own before the day's end. But she couldn't let Miken keep going.

"These men would kill you if they could," he said. His breaths were still heavy from the fight. She could see his blood pounding through his neck, hot and ready to do more. "They've already tried."

"Then you're no better than them."

His cold, focused eyes searched hers. He had already killed too many men. She needed his blood to cool before he'd hear her.

"I need to clear the archers," Miken said.

He brushed past her and she stiffened at the feeling of it. Then she heard his feet stop. He finally saw Melony. The two of them stood with stiff, defensive frames. Miken didn't smile at her. He didn't go to her with open arms and embrace her and welcome her back. Even if he'd just welcomed her back then Alexria could have breathed easier. Instead Miken stood inspecting Melony. He slowly shifted his shoulders in a way to make himself taller and more sturdy.

"Lerato," Miken said. His voice was cold. "I want her tied up and stored in the bottom of the ship until I get there."

Alexria closed her eyes. What had she brought Melony into?

"Who is she to you?" Lerato asked. He had to have known she was considered the Duke's daughter. He had to have recognized that much.

"Desalian."

One word. That was all it took to state Miken's opinion. His lack of trust.

Miken pulled his mask back over his face and started down the passage away from the docks, to wherever he'd find the archers. And he was ready to do it alone. Melony lowered her eyes as he passed her.

Alexria drew her sword again. She was becoming tired. Her medicine would only last for so long before it faded. But then, Miken's strength could fade just as easily. And it seemed he wouldn't care if it did.

"Alex, let him go," Lerato said.

But Alexria started in a jog after Miken. "He'll get himself killed if I do that."

* * * * *

"Lerato!"

Genev embraced him when he reached her. Lerato groaned at the weight of pain it caused his back and Genev jumped away from him when she heard it.

Her wide eyes looked him over. "You look terrible. What did they do to you?"

Lerato forced his tall posture to assure her he was better than he looked. The jog from his cell to here had felt long, during which his beaten back had done nothing other than complain. Between himself and the injured Knight, their pace had been slower than it should have been. Genev's embrace had brought back the throbbing of his lashes, though that was not something she needed to know.

"I'll be alright," he said. "Why aren't you on the ship?"

Genev bit her lip and looked out at the docks. "They're trying."

The ship wasn't ready yet. There was only a handful of Hydians onboard that Lerato could see. Each of them carried a shield over their heads as arrows showered down from higher up in the fortress. Here inside the cave was the only chance of shelter from it. All the Desalians that had been in the cave were either dead or bound under Hydian guard. The Hydians in the cave were scrambling for chainmail, shields, or any other kinds of armour they could find on the bodies of their enemies. Kaytan stood at the water's edge directing Knights and sailors into a row boat. The men were arranging what few shields they had to create a safe tent above themselves during their row.

The Knight guarding Genev spoke up. "I'd wager that if we don't get this ship moving soon, we'll be cornered off by land *and* sea."

"Yet we have no offense against archers who stand out of reach," Genev said. She looked as though she were near tears.

"Miken and Alex promised to clear them," Lerato said.

Genev looked at Lerato and then over the group he had arrived with. "Alexria isn't with you?"

"It was her choice to go."

"How will they return in time to join us? We can't afford to wait."

Lerato had no answer. His hope was that Miken knew how to navigate this island. Regardless of how reckless he appeared, he had to know another escape.

"Climb a rope to them."

It was the girl, Melony, who spoke. It surprised Lerato to hear it.

"Climb?" he asked.

"The side of the mountain," she said as though he should have known the answer to his own question. "I can do it."

Just this morning Melony had been among those who had captured them. It felt odd to have her here. Lerato hadn't yet asked Alexria about what had happened back in the prison hallway. There was certainly more to it than swaying the mind of an enemy.

"Let me prove you can trust me," Melony said.

Lerato nodded. They didn't have time to consider it long. "Oversee her," he said to one of the Knights with them. He would have done so himself, but he doubted he had the strength for it.

Melony jogged out onto the stone slab of the dock. Some barrels stood off to the side and she gathered a long rope out of one.

Kaytan noticed them and called out to the Knight with her. The Knight mentioned Lerato. That was when Kaytan noticed Lerato.

"She's the Duke's daughter," Kaytan said as he joined them.

"Miken and Alex are clearing archers," Lerato said, watching Melony instead of Kaytan's reaction. "The girl says she can help."

Melony handed one end of the rope to the Knight and tied the other to her belt. She brushed her hands on the ground, rubbed them together, and walked toward the closest wall of the cave.

"Then they must have beaten the sense out of you too," Kaytan said. "She's Desalian. She has no reason to help us."

Lerato nodded slowly as he watched her. "Alex seems to trust her. Miken seems not to."

"And you?"

Melony started climbing up the rock in a way Lerato had never seen before. Her fingers and toes sought out the smallest ledges to grip to and she moved across it as though she were crawling on a floor. It was like watching a squirrel on a tree or a spider on a pillar, only she moved with skilled grace. The higher she climbed the more Lerato wanted to tell the girl to get down, but the more he also wanted to see her succeed in whatever she was trying to do. This was, after all, her home.

"I'm curious," Lerato said.

* * * * *

For most of their sprint through the fortress, Alexria thought Miken hadn't noticed her following him. He didn't acknowledge her or glance back to check that she kept up. It wasn't until he killed a Desalian armed with a quiver that he spoke to her.

"You'll need these," he said, handing her more arrows to add to her quiver.

His pace only slowed when he climbed stairs or turned sharp corners or when their path was blocked by Desalians. Alexria followed as close to him as she could as he wound through the passages. A path of wounded men lay behind them, sending a warning to others in the area. When he came to a sudden stop, Alexria almost ran into the back of him. Their chests were heaving. Miken snuffed out the nearby torches with their caps and peered around a corner into the next passage. After a long moment he turned back to Alexria.

"We'll follow that passage for twenty strides and then turn left," Miken said quietly. He used his dagger to tear the sleeve off his shirt and cut in into a long strip of cloth. "That passage opens up to the wall surrounding the fortress. The archers bombarding the ship will be there. We only need to keep that section clear long enough for the ship to set sail."

He wrapped the cloth like a mask over Alexria's mouth and nose, as he had, and began tying it behind her neck. Alexria held her hair out of the way.

"We'll find a way out after that," he said.

"We both will," Alexria added.

This brought his eyes to hers for the first time since they started running. It was only the flicker of a glance, difficult to see in the darkness they stood in. A break in his military series of thoughts.

"I'd have no one to dance with otherwise," Alexria said.

"You can dance fine without me," Miken said as he finished tying the mask.

"Mike."

He looked at her this time. The fierce eyes she had seen earlier had softened, even just for now. The face of a warrior would return the moment they stepped out that passage and into the daylight. But beneath it, somewhere, there would still be the man she knew.

"Are you ready?" he asked.

No. Stepping out into the open in Desali territory was something she'd never be ready for. But she gave a small nod.

If it weren't for Miken leading her forward she may not have moved. Yet she followed with a bow in one hand and a quiver of arrows on her back. While Miken ran out into the daylight with his sword swinging, Alexria stopped on the edge of the passage and released arrow after arrow. Each strike she made was like weaving a needle around Miken's movements. Like an elaborate dance. He never flinched. He swayed up and down and side to side slashing at soldiers and throwing them down to the houses within the fortress walls. He blocked arrows with the bodies of his enemies and she'd time arrows to weave around him and strike down the threats. It wasn't until she was out of arrows that Alexria drew her sword, dropping the bow and quiver where she stood. There were few archers left now. Alexria struck down two more while Miken handled the rest. As Alexria turned to check for other threats she saw someone else coming. Not from along the passage as she'd expected, but climbing up the mountain face.

"Melony?"

There was nowhere to climb up from. The only thing beneath them besides the docks was the ocean, and they were nearly as high as the ship's mast. Melony's hands were on the wall's ledge. She adjusted her footing, stretched a knee up to the solid surface, then curled a leg to the safe side of the wall. A rope was tied to her belt and it stretched all the way down to the ship. She'd brought them their way out.

A man sprung from the passage Alexria and Miken had just come from. He struck Melony hard across the face and it knocked her over. She fell, slipping to the side, back toward the drop she'd just climbed. Alexria reached for her. She caught Melony's rope as it pulled taut. The man grabbed Alexria by the hair, but she kept both hands gripping the rope. The smack of metal on metal could be heard behind her. Miken was here, his sword drawn and held against the blade of the man.

"Miken," the man said, partially in warning, partially in an odd greeting.

"Adicara," Miken said through his teeth. "Release them or I'll kill you right here."

"That's not the first time you've promised that," Adicara said. "Yet I'm still here."

The rope was cutting into Alexria's palms and fingers and her side was beginning to ache again. The rope swayed over the wall's edge to wherever Melony hung. This couldn't happen again. She couldn't lose Allia again, whether she was Melony or not. She'd rather have the rope pull herself over the cliff with her daughter than let go. Adicara could pull at her hair all he wanted. It wouldn't make any difference. Not this time.

Then Melony's hand reached up to the wall's ledge again. Alexria let herself breathe. That strong, dust-covered hand, her little girl's hand, was pulling herself to safety.

Adicara released Alexria and started at Miken with sword swinging. The clash of swords was a fast paced rhythm.

Melony lifted her elbow up to the ledge and her face appeared. Her eyes held a fiery purpose. Alexria reached to Melony's arm with one hand and kept a tight grip of the rope with the other. Melony climbed over the wall's ledge and sat down on the safe side of it. Her chest heaved up and down. She looked at the fight between Miken and Adicara.

Alexria put a hand on the side of Melony's face. "Are you alright?"

Melony looked at her and nodded. She started back up to her feet. She had a stubborn strength, just as Alexria and Miken both did.

"Melony, listen to me," Alexria said. "You need to secure the rope and climb back down to the ship."

Melony was watching the fight again. The sound of metal was the only sound in the air. It was sure to attract more Desalian men.

"Can you do that?" Alexria asked.

Melony nodded again and started untying the rope tied to her belt. "Are you coming?"

In the background, past the wall, the ship's sails billowed and began to move. How long until the rope wouldn't reach the ship anymore?

"We'll follow soon," Alexria said. "But you need to go."

Alexria took up her own sword again and went to help Miken. Adicara must have heard her coming, or expected her to come, because his sword blocked the first swing she made. She blocked a swing toward her knees. As Adicara threw an elbow back into Miken's face, she swept her sword up to Adicara's side, but he blocked it before she could strike flesh. Miken was stumbling back from the strike. Adicara's sword focused on her. His quick strokes from one side then the other made Alexria's sword feel rushed. Sloppy. She kept taking steps backwards. Miken joined them, taking pressure off her, but not slowing Adicara. They'd made no strikes against him. No cuts of a blade or strikes of a fist. Yet Adicara continually knocked down one of them while he faced the other. It was a fist across her temple the first time she was knocked back, then a knee to her stomach which she'd manage to see coming and tighten her stomach at least somewhat to lighten the blow. She had been slower to get up from that one. Then soon after that was the kick to her side, her wounded side, which sent her low to the ground. It was after this one that turned her side's ache into a sharp pain. She heard Miken drop after that. His sword clattered to the stone behind him as he fell to his knees and then was kicked to fall backwards. Adicara's sword pulled back for a killing stroke, his back to Alexria. Alexria lunged herself forward to push Adicara off the ledge he stood close to. She could only reach his knees, but she let her weight pull him down. Adicara tumbled and rolled off the wall to the houses below.

Miken was up again, his sword restless in his hand, looking down at where Adicara lay far out of reach. Further down the wall, still out of range, more Desalians were charging in their direction. Melony had already climbed down the rope to the ship. Alexria tried to lift herself off her knees but the pain that lashed out through her side was too much. Darkness threatened to sweep over her eyes but then recovered.

"Mike," Alexria said, hoping to draw his attention. Even to herself, her voice sounded weak.

He wanted to jump down to Adicara. Alexria could see the ache in him to finish it. For so long he'd wanted to finish it. But the Desalians were getting closer. The ship was getting further.

"Killing him won't erase anything," Alexria said.

He didn't turn. The pain in Alexria's side was beginning to throb again. It weakened her. Even holding herself up on her knees took effort. But Miken didn't seem to notice. It was as if he was back at their home fifteen years ago, staring into the darkness after Adicara.

"Mike, I can't fight anymore."

This time Miken looked at her. It was as though looking at her, seeing her, snapped him back to clear thinking. He took her in with a glance, looked back at Adicara, then sheathed his sword. When he lifted Alexria to her feet she grimaced at the pain it caused her. She swayed for a step before catching her balance. Miken pulled out a folded glove that had been tucked in his belt. He straddled the wall next to where the rope was secured, held it with his gloved hand, and extended the other hand to her. It wasn't until she looked out at the ship, at how taut the rope was becoming between them and where they needed to be, that Alexria realized how far down they needed to slide. And the escaping Hydians continued to drift further away.

Alexria took Miken's hand and sat in front of him, letting her feet dangle over the edge. This was the same ledge that Melony had almost fallen off of. It was a far drop, at least five counts to fall to the bottom. Miken wrapped an arm around her and pushed themselves off. The rope sagged to an even steeper drop down to the ship. She felt like her stomach had been pulled up into her throat. Wind rushed past her face and blew her hair back. The rope hissed through Miken's gloved hand. She opened her eyes again. She was approaching the ship fast.

Then the rope was cut limp behind them. They dropped down. Miken held her tighter. Alexria could barely gasp before her feet struck the water hard. The water slapped her hip before engulfing her. The cold stole the air from her. She wanted to breathe. Wanted to swim up toward air. But Miken had a tight grip on both her and on the rope. The water rushed past them like a current as they were dragged behind the ship. Her head was throbbing the same way her side was. The surface drew closer. The hull of the ship was like a nearing shadow in front of them. Alexria's head felt as though it were spinning. Waves churned above them and soon they were pulled up and out of them, out of the water, into an inviting breath of air. Miken continued to grip the rope with one hand and her with the other as they were pulled up the ship's stern. Her head continued to throb. Her grip around Miken's shoulder's weakened. The view around her was becoming dark, the sounds becoming more distant. Then the darkness that had been threatening to sweep over her eyes finally took over.

Chapter 20

An Old Memory

2 years before the shipwreck

"Everything is as you left it," was a humble statement. If that had been true then the floor and furniture and cushions and clothes would all have been caked in dust after thirteen years of waiting. Instead Alexria and Miken walked into their clean home. Not the kind of clean that comes from a quick sweep and dust the day before, but the clean from years of maintaining the sweeping and dusting. Thirteen years of sweeping and dusting an empty home that didn't plan to be returned to.

Nevik lit the fireplace by passing on the flame of his lantern to kindling. He arranged the larger logs and the smaller pieces so the fire would build on its own. Seeing the firelight was soothing for Alexria, but it couldn't loosen the churning knot of emotion in her stomach and her throat. She couldn't even explain what the emotion was. It wasn't fear or excitement or sorrow or relief. Maybe a blend of them all. And others, even, that she couldn't put a word to.

Miken returned from upstairs with dry clothes and Nevik left them alone. Alexria had almost forgotten she was cold. Perhaps that was why she felt so tense. Changing into the dry clothes helped her to breathe easier. She still shivered. Her fingers were still white and aching as they tried to warm-up. Miken wrapped her in a blanket and sat with her on the cushioned bench in front of the fire. Miken held her tight to settle her shivering and Alexria hugged his arms around herself. The fire snapped and crackled. They used to sit here often. Sometimes with one child or the other or both. Or sometimes just the two of them as they did now. It was here that so many stories were told and moments were shared and laughter was sung out with smiles. It was also here where Miken had fought with Adicara. The storm pelted rain against the house and the wind howled in gusts. Their bedroom, where Alexria had faced Adicara, was upstairs. But to explore their house tonight felt haunting and dark.

"What do we do now?" Alexria asked.

Miken kissed her temple from where he sat behind her. "Just sleep. I'm here."

Sleeping was easier than Alexria thought it would be. Her eyes were heavy. Her body ached. She listened to the voice of the fireplace warming her and the persistent storm outside. She slipped away into dreams. She was with Allia again. The small girl crawled with quick, definite movements. An open mouthed smile lifted her baby cheeks. She plopped down on her bottom and stretched her arms up. Alexria scooped her child into her arms and rocked her. The daughter fit well in her mother's arms. Alexria undid her necklace and dangled the shiny pendent above Allia's reach. Allia waved her hands up at it and then Alexria lowered the necklace so her daughter could have the satisfaction of grabbing hold. Her daughter smiled. Alexria smiled.

Then the room became cast over in shadows as the curtains closed. Rough hands grabbed her from behind. An Etimire pounced into view and hissed at her, bearing its teeth. A cloth was gripped over Alexria's mouth and she breathed a terrible stench. Allia cried. The hands held her, trapped her. Struggling against it felt useless. Calling out wasn't possible.

Alexria suddenly sat up and Allia was gone. The man was gone. She was on the cushioned bench with Miken. She was panting. Her dream had woken Miken too and he reached an assuring hand to hers. She leaned back against Miken, closed her eyes, and breathed.

The fireplace glowed with red embers. The room itself was brightened instead by the light creeping in from outside. The storm had passed.

"We need to go upstairs, don't we?" Alexria asked. She wanted him to say 'no.' To say 'not now' or 'the next time we visit the house.'

"I was already there last night," Miken said.

Alexria had forgotten that he would have needed to go there to gather dry clothes. "What's it like?"

"Quiet," he said. "Like it had been that way for a while."

'Quiet' wasn't a bad word. It made it sound possible to face.

"It should be better this morning," Miken said.

It would be cold upstairs, making it harder to leave the warm air of the fireplace and Miken's embrace and the blanket. Yet she started with setting the blanket aside and lifting herself up. The staircase looked as though it climbed up into darkness. As she neared it, she noticed the faint glow of daylight at the top. The light took some of the intimidation away and helped carry herself up. Miken's steps were close behind her.

The curtain at the far end of the hall swayed in the breeze, letting flickers of daylight sneak through. The first door, the one to their old room, was wide open to let the air move. The room was more dim than it was dark. Along the first wall was the long flat cupboard where they had kept clothes and blankets folded in the drawers. Beside it, in the corner, was the wardrobe where dresses and cloaks hung. She couldn't even remember which clothes she had left behind and chose not to come back for. She was sure she'd recognize them, though, when she brought herself to look.

Then there was the bed. The curved headboard stood sturdy against the wall opposite the door and the bed itself came out toward them. This was the last place she and Miken and Laren had sat together. Alexria could picture the three of them sitting there, little Laren in the middle. It was the night they had lost Allia and the night they had lost their third child. The next morning, the plague would finally take Laren from them as well. But on that night, for that moment, they were together. She could remember the feeling of Laren's weak frame laying against her as though it had only happened last night. A tear escaped from her eye. Miken went to the nightstand, picked up a book that lay there, and blew the light dust off the top. He opened it to the marked page.

"Is it the story from that night?" Alexria asked.

Miken nodded slowly. He turned the pages back and forth. "We read a lot with him that night." He lowered himself to the edge of the bed when he settled on a page. "*The other Guardians of Hydia did not see them leave and, by the time they noticed, Alecan and Arimon were already half-way to the docks. The two men kept hidden from the patrols by following the shaded streets and moving through crowds*"

Miken turned the page. Alexria started toward him. Laren had loved stories of the Guardians of Hydia. He always asked for them.

"*The two men agreed with the others that the plan was not the most wise. The chances of returning were low. The chances of success were even lower.*"

Alexria reached the bed and sat next to Miken, sinking into the comfort of the blankets. She leaned her head on his shoulder. He looped an arm around her waist as he read on. She could feel more tears swelling in her eyes. She could hear Miken's voice struggling.

"*Yet if they succeeded, the Desalians could finally be driven out of the Capital. And so they smuggled themselves onto the ship and set off across the ocean. The Capital and everything familiar to them slowly drifted further and further away, leaving them bound for places unknown. It was said that no Hydian who set foot on the islands of Desali has ever returned. Alecan and Arimon, however, were convinced it could be done. The two men were young enough to believe with a child's faith that the unaccomplished was not impossible.*"

Miken stopped reading. His voice was choking up too much. Alexria kissed his cheek and found the skin wet and tasted like salt.

"He always asked what 'unaccomplished' was," Miken said in a quiet voice. "Every time."

Alexria hugged him tight and Miken curled his embrace around her.

"What did you tell him?" she asked gently.

He took a long sigh before he answered. "Something no one's ever done before. Not even the Guardians of Hydia."

This made Alexria smile. "He would have been a smart boy."

"He was certainly curious enough to be."

Hollers and whistles came from outside. The kinds that came from urging horses and coordinating yard work. Both Alexria and Miken flinched at the sudden noise. She had expected their home to be still and quiet with only a couple servants tending to it for them. These sounds were from a crowd.

Miken stood first and went to the curtained balcony. Alexria followed so she could stay close to him. The curtains swayed as though part of a soft dance. Sunlight glowed along the edges on either side. Miken pushed it aside with an open hand. Alexria winced as the morning flooded into the room. She blinked several times, adjusting to the new light, before looking out at the view.

The courtyard was wet and dripping. A pair of small birds fluttered from landing to landing, pecking at bugs and drinking from puddles as they went. Chimney smoke spiralled up from the servant's house. Aside from that there was no other movement in the courtyard. Yet beyond it, past the servant's house and outside the wall, was where all the noise came from. It was in the direction of the barn. They couldn't see much from the balcony. It wasn't until they went down to the courtyard and out the open gate that they saw the team of work horses and men. The horses were hitched to an old tree trunk, straining to pull it out of the ground. Some men were digging at the trunk with shovels and axes. Others were at the tree which had been cut to fall away from the barn. These men worked at chopping the wood and stacking it onto wagons.

A few of the men raised their arms or hats in greeting to Alexria and Miken. "Good morning!" they called.

Miken returned the gesture.

In the work there was sweat and smiles and aching muscles and laughter. There was life here. After all the years they'd been gone, after all that had been lost, there was still life here. Alexria could still breathe easy here.

* * * * *

Most of the servants that had lived here thirteen years ago had stayed. Miken recognized these faces and the servants recognized him, as well as Alexria. When evening came, all the working men left to return home except the familiar faces. A long table was brought out to the courtyard and a generous meal was served. Miken and Alexria were told it was a toast to a long awaited return. The pig that had been roasting all afternoon was carved and served. Fresh loaves of bread were cut into slices and new jars of jam were opened. Vegetables of all kinds laid out on platters. Some had been steamed and seasoned while others were raw and arranged like flat bouquets. Wine and sweetened tea were poured.

Stories were told all through the dinner and well after. Miken and Alexria listened. They were the kinds of stories that lifted spirits and brought both smiles and laughter. They were stories from the past thirteen years. Some of the stories appeared well known, for whoever was telling it continued to be interrupted by other versions or missing details. Yet it was all in good fun. It made the stars come out faster than it seemed they should, and still the entertainment went on.

Finally Nevik stood and raised his cup high. "A toast," he said, "before the evening ends."

The table quieted and the servants took their cups in their hands. Crickets could be heard in the field.

"To Sir Miken and Lady Alexria," Nevik said. "May they forever be in the Greater Power's care. And may they no longer be strangers in their own home."

The words brought warm smiles and light laughter as they all drank to the toast. Then Miken stood with his cup in hand before the conversations had much chance to build again. He wasn't sure why he did. He couldn't remember the last time he'd made a toast. It was as though his instincts told him to. As he looked over the men and women and Alexria all waiting for whatever he had to say, he remembered that he had always done this. For any festive occasion when they'd pull out the table and dine with everyone in the household, Miken had always been the one to close with a toast. He wasn't sure where to begin, but he began anyway.

"To all of you," he said slowly. "For your generous hospitality and for keeping this home and these fields longer than I think we expected of you. You all need to be thanked for that." He paused with a brief glance to Alexria. "To this home and all the life and the memories within it." He looked down at his cup and took a breath before he went on. "To Laren. For those four bright years we were given to share with him. To our youngest. May the child remain a sweet angel in our eyes. To Allia." Miken thought of Melony when he said the name and he did his best not to pause. "May her sweet soul be in the Greater Power's care."

He looked at Alexria again. Her eyes wore a warm, moist smile.

"And to Alex," he said. There weren't enough words to say what he needed to. Her patience, her love, her endurance, her strength, her weaknesses, her loyalty, her heart... But as he looked at her now, with her soft smile, he didn't need the words for her to know. "To you, Alex," he said quietly, just for her.

Miken raised his cup and drank a sip from it. The servants followed, giving quiet words of approval. Alexria thanked him in a voice too quiet for him to hear.

"They're good people," Alexria said after everyone had retired for the night. The light of their fireplace glowed on her face. "I'd like to visit more."

Miken had been sharing the same thoughts. They wouldn't be staying here long. It wasn't that they were running from this home again. This home, these people, and these joys were good for them. The days of running from it were fading away. For the first time in so long, Miken felt... he felt full. Perhaps content was the word. Alexria showed that same contentment. For the first time they weren't leaving because their aching hearts pleaded them to. They would leave because they chose to. Because hearts were finally filled. And this time they'd return home more often.

Miken kissed her cheek. "I'd like that."

Chapter 21

Course Charted

After the shipwreck

After Miken and Alexria were safely pulled on board the ship, Miken gathered her limp body up in his arms. The bed in the Captain's quarters was the only decent one that Miken could think of, so that was where he carried Alexria to. Genev was already seated on it but, when she saw Alexria, she stood without being asked to. He laid Alexria down as gently as he could. She was drenched with ocean water, like himself. Her forehead was cold. He undid the bandage around Alexria's side to find that her wound appeared clean. The scab was a deep red with no unwanted colours mixed into it. The skin around it looked like healthy skin without the expected ring of red in the area of the scab. The Balus Root medicine had worked well. It was the other medicine, the one that had brought her strength back just long enough to fight through the fortress, that must have worn off. Perhaps sleep was best for her now.

"Can I ask a favour, my Lady?" Miken said, without turning his eyes off Alexria. He wrapped the bandage back over the wound.

"I have no skill in treating injuries," Genev said.

"I need you to watch her for me," Miken said. Alexria's face was so peaceful when she slept. "She can't be alone when she wakes up."

"Where will you be?" Genev asked.

Miken laid a dry blanket over Alexria and stood. Genev stood with a stiff stature and with her arms wrapped around herself. He may have considered explaining the situation of Melony to Lerato, but he couldn't tell Genev now. She had already seen enough in the last few days to overwhelm her.

"You can have your brother replace you if you like," he said. "I'll be back soon."

He wanted to leave before she had a chance to say 'no,' but this time he waited for a nod to be sure she'd be staying.

She hesitated, but agreed. "I'll fetch dry clothes as well."

"Thank-you, my Lady," he said.

He found Melony on the starboard side of the ship watching Petayrn as they sailed around and away from it. The ship was busy with the shouts of the Captain's orders and the sailors following them. The Hydian Knights watched the island and surrounding waters for Desalian ships readying an attempt to pursue them. Miken's work was done. They'd reach the safety of Hydia's shore and maybe even meet with other Hydian ships on the way. Their escape had caught the Desalians off guard enough to keep Miken from worrying of further capture.

"We need to talk," Miken said to Melony. His words startled her enough to make her flinch. "Below deck."

Miken led her to the belly of the ship among all the storage crates and barrels, where they'd have the privacy to speak. Enough light shone through the wooden boards above them to make the space dim. Melony kept a few steps behind him. It was a safe distance for her to stand at, whether she intended it that way or not. To him, she wasn't his daughter. He had to keep reminding himself of that. She was Desalian.

"It seems we have a problem," he said.

"You more than me." She spoke with more confidence than was good for her.

Miken gave a half-amused, half-irritated smile. "You should remember, Melony, that you're on *my* territory now. You play by *my* rules." He pointed to the wooden hull in the direction of the island. "And if Alexria didn't trust you, I'd already have you overboard swimming back to your little island by now. And I doubt you'd survive the trip."

She was smart not to say anything back, but her strong stature was still present. Feet could be heard on the wood above them, filling in the brief silence. The ship creaked and rocked.

"Why are you onboard?" he said.

"You ordered me to."

"No, I ordered you bound in the bottom of the ship. But you had a chance to leave since then," he said. His words sounded harsh to even himself. "So why are you here?" He leaned back against a crate and folded his arms.

"Curious."

"About?"

"Why she saved my life."

"Hm." Miken gave a slow nod and the same amused smile again. "You climbed the mountain *before* she saved your life. You'll have to lie better than you are if you want me to believe you."

"I wouldn't lie to you, sir." She said the word 'sir' with such distaste that it took away any sympathy he had for her.

"Every Desalian lies for survival," Miken said. "I, for example, have spent the last fifteen years gaining the trust of Hydia's royalty. Duke Sular wasn't going to ruin that for me. Even if that meant killing some of his men. And I certainly won't have a little girl like yourself ruin my work."

"Is being a Guardian of Hydia part of your work?" she asked in challenge.

Miken's chin tipped to the side at those words. Adicara was the most likely to know that information. Miken took a long, slow breath before speaking again. "Who told you that?"

Her slight hesitation was her mistake. "Anyone could figure that out."

"You spent you're entire life on Petayrn. You have no way of proving that fact unless someone told you or someone warned you about me."

Miken watched Melony's jaw become tense in frustration. She said nothing. He couldn't accuse her of trusting Adicara unless she admitted it. It wasn't that he cared. If Melony wanted to trust the same man who kidnapped her all those years ago, than let her trust him. Let her be his puppet. If that was the game Adicara wanted to play, Miken would take part in it.

"Who told you?" Miken asked. He began closing the distance between her and him with slow steps.

"No one did." Her strength was beginning to weaken in her eyes and her stature.

"I want a name."

"I didn't hear it from anyone."

Her stubbornness grew his frustration into anger. If Adicara thought he could hide his eyes behind a girl, he was wrong. "A name."

She shook her head. "There is none."

Miken flashed his dagger up to threaten her neck. "*Don't* lie to me."

Melony stumbled back into the barrel behind her. Miken's dagger followed her neck. Her eyes shone wide in shock and fear and then squeezed closed. She was trembling. Her breaths, her arms, her mouth... all of her was trembling. He had seen those fear-filled eyes before. Years ago, when she was only a child, Miken could remember sitting through an evening thunderstorm with Alexria, Laren, and Allia. The fireplace warmed the room in a way that helped soften the rolling thunder outside. He could remember a loud snap of thunder and made Laren jump and Alexria flinch at the surprise of it. Allia's little eyes had opened wide in fear. Miken had scooped her up then. Now, Miken could only lighten the pressure of the blade.

"I couldn't kill her," Melony said, keeping her eyes closed. Even her voice shook. "I had a shot back in the fortress. Her and the Hydians. And the Prince. I should have taken it but I couldn't. Because of her I couldn't." She swallowed. "I want to know why."

Miken assumed she spoke of Alexria. He took the dagger away and walked around the barrel so their backs were to each other. He felt his hand begin to tremble the way she was and he pressed it to his chin. Her eyes had burned in his mind. Whether Melony was here as a spy or not, whether she had just lied to him or not, Miken believed her. He wanted to believe her.

"Get back up on deck," Miken said quietly. "And don't make any mistakes."

She left without hesitation. Miken listened to her boots on the wood until she reached the steps bending up to the deck. There she stopped. It was quiet for a moment.

"You're my father, aren't you?" Melony asked. "If she's my mother."

Miken wanted to think she'd figured that out on her own, the way a clever kid would. But he couldn't get Adicara out of his mind. He couldn't help but wonder how much influence he'd had and how much he'd told her.

"You should leave when you're told to," Miken said.

This time she did.

* * * * *

The First Mate, now appointed as Captain, spun the wheel and the ship veered left to circle behind the island's mountain. The jagged stone loomed high over the ship's mast. Kaytan jogged up to join Lerato and the Captain.

"We've only seen one Desalian ship so far," Kaytan said, "but it was still scrambling to come after us."

"And the wind will be in our favour," the Captain said.

"There will still be plenty of Desalians at sea," Lerato said. The daylight would keep any Desalian ships from creeping up on them, as they had the first time. Yet Lerato could picture the same series of events occurring again to bring them back into chains.

"There'll be Hydians at sea too," Kaytan said. There was a faint smile in his expression. He looked much more hopeful than Lerato was. "I'd wager, by now, at least a fleet of Hydian ships have been sent out in search of us. It won't be long before we'll have friendly escorts."

Lerato had forgotten about the chance of a search coming to their aid. After so long of looking over his shoulder for enemies, it had become an easy habit.

"You can rest now, Sir," the Captain said to Lerato. "You've long been needing it."

Lerato couldn't bring himself to retreat completely. Instead he followed the steps to the main deck and sat on the second-last step. The ocean breeze was soothing for a change. He breathed it in. He'd never imagined himself as someone who could escape a Desalian island and yet here he was. He was weak and sore, but he had still done it.

The girl, Melony, came up from below deck. It still felt out of place to see her here. Just as Lerato was considering putting her under watch of Hydian Knight, Miken came up from the same direction she had. His steps were slow and heavy. He looked at Melony as though there were no one else on board except her. He stood where he was with his arms folded and then leaned a wall, watching her.

"Miken," Lerato said, calling his attention to him.

Miken barely acknowledged him.

"Are you alright?" Lerato asked.

Miken took a long breath. "I'm still alive. That's a start." He pushed himself away from the wall and started pacing.

"And Alex?"

Miken nodded. "She'll be fine." Miken's gaze glanced toward the upper deck as he paced and this stopped him. He paused for a long moment before speaking again.

"Is that your Captain?" Miken asked.

Lerato glanced at them. "Our Captain was killed when we crashed. The First Mate filled the position."

Miken was quiet again. He stared up at the new Captain as though solving a puzzle.

"Have you met him before?" Lerato asked.

"Several times," Miken said. "On the shoreline of Hydia." He paused again, then added, "He'll get us home safe."

* * * * *

Alexria woke from the gentle touch of a hand taking hers. While the throbbing of her head and the pain in her side and the ache of shoulders and legs all made her want to keep her eyes closed, it was the touch of the hand that invited her to wake. The touch was warm and the fingers curled around under her palm. She could feel the texture of calluses from someone who didn't fear work.

She heard a quiet voice. Miken's voice. "Could you give us a moment?"

She opened her eyes, allowing the darkness to be brushed away. She blinked at the new light. Miken was seated next to her and he lifted her hand to his lips to kiss it. They were in a room. The cabin of a ship that rocked and swayed to the sound of the ocean outside. The memories of Petayrn came back quick.

"Desalians?" she asked in a stale voice.

Miken stroked his hand through her hair. "We're safe," he said. "We're on our way back to the Capital."

Alexria breathed and nodded. On their way back. It was good to hear those words for a change.

"How are you feeling?" Miken asked.

Alexria shifted as though she were to get up, but everything ached from fatigue and strain. She gave a weak smile. "I think I may stay here a little longer."

Miken also offered a weak smile, but it looked as though there was a touch of pain behind it. He could only nod. His gaze was more on her hand than it was on her. She lifted her hand to his face and stroked the texture of his cheek. He closed his eyes at the touch.

"What is it?" she asked.

He took a long breath in and let it out slow. He started shaking his head. "I can't do it, Alex," he said. "I can't do it."

"You can't do what?" Alexria asked. She kept her hand on his cheek and stiffly lifted herself up to her elbow.

He winced before he even brought the words out. And when he did the words were so quiet and hoarse that Alexria could feel the pain behind them. "I threatened her."

He didn't need to say the name Melony or Allia for Alexria to know what he meant.

"What kind of man does that?" he asked. "What kind of man threatens a *child?*"

He opened his eyes to look at her. What could she say to a gaze that was broken? She couldn't say she didn't want to hear about what happened. She couldn't say it wouldn't happen again. She didn't want it to, and she would do all she could to make sure it didn't, but she couldn't bring herself to believe it. So instead of speaking, Alexria lifted her shoulders up off the bed, with more effort than she thought it would take, and sat closer to him.

"I want to believe her," he said. "I want to, I just..." He shook his head and gave up with the words.

Alexria rubbed her free hand along his shoulders and kissed his temple. "We've gone through worse," she said softly. "We'll get through this too. You and me."

"How?" He leaned his head against hers. He was more weak than she was. His wounds were deeper.

Alexria thought for a long moment. She couldn't even picture how it would be after they 'get through this.' She couldn't imagine what their 'good' will be. "I don't know," she said. "But I think we're still young enough to believe with a child's faith that the unaccomplished is not impossible."

Miken's smile was weak, but it was there. That was a start.

"And I'm told," Alexria said, "that means no one's ever done it before. Not even the Guardians of Hydia." She kissed his cheek and, when he leaned into it, she let it linger. He smelled like the ocean. "I only hope the Greater Power will help us somehow."

Miken took a long breath. "I think He always has."

Look for Book Two in the Guardians of Hydia series:

Hidden Shadows.

Hidden Shadows

Prologue

Another arrow struck the heart of the target, forcing through the others already cluttered there. After speaking to the Hydian prisoners, and specifically to 'the maid,' Melony retreated to the nearby training square. She moved a painted target into the hall so she could use her bow. She'd let Sinele deal with the prisoners however he wanted to. She didn't care anymore. She wanted all this to be over. She drew another arrow.

"Melony?"

It was the cautious voice of her sister, Melinda. Or could they even be called sisters anymore? Melony drew back her bowstring.

"What happened?" Melinda asked from where she stood behind her.

Melony paused, holding her aim steady. Today was supposed to be simple. They were only supposed to hunt down the remaining Hydians on their island and then use them as bargaining chips. Nothing more.

"I'm a Hydian," Melony said. She released the arrow, once again striking the target's heart. The words sounded worse when she said them. Hydians were a weak, pathetic people.

Melinda was left speechless at first. "How...? What does that mean?"

Melony turned away from her target and shook her head. Her fists were all clenched up. "It shouldn't make sense," she said. "I mean, if I were being played then none of it should make any sense."

"What shouldn't make sense?"

Melony pointed in the direction of the prison. "The so-called 'Hydian maid,' the one caught in the forest,... she thinks I'm hers."

Melinda stared at her as though she had spoken in a foreign tongue. She took a small step back and thought for a moment before she said anything. "What did Father say?"

Melony gave an annoyed laugh. "He won't admit that. He'd never say that the last eighteen years of my life were a lie. Or maybe seventeen years. I don't even know how old I am anymore." It was hard to imagine her 'Father,' Duke Sular, being the type of man to kidnap a child. But maybe he had been a more capable man back then. Or maybe he hired someone else to do it.

"But then how do you know you're Hydian?" Melinda asked.

"Because she has this." Melony dug into her pocket for the necklace and tossed it to Melinda. "She has the exact same one." She turned back to her archery target. In a way she wished she had never noticed the necklace on the woman. She wished she never had a second thought about it.

"Did she offer to bring you to Hydia?" Melinda asked.

Melony snapped her eyes back to Melinda. "What?"

Melinda gave a weak shrug. "Does she want you back?"

"I can't go to Hydia," Melony snapped. "Why would I ever want to go there?"

Melinda glanced up and down the hall and then stepped closer. "Because if I had a chance to leave Desali, I would."

"Why?" Melony asked, keeping her words sharp. "We're a strong kingdom."

"We're a blood-hungry kingdom." Melinda sounded as though she wanted to scream it but couldn't bring her voice above a whisper. "And it'll get you killed."

"By who?" Melony couldn't argue the 'blood-hungry' part. She had heard enough stories and seen enough examples.

"Sinele would."

The words silenced Melony. At first she wanted to deny the possibility, but she couldn't bring herself to. Sinele had always been the one to step on her or push her aside. He wouldn't be the first Desalian to turn a blade against his own family. Every year he became more capable of it.

The distant sound of a battle caught Melony's ear. It came from the direction of the prison cells.

"Melony," Melinda said, pressing the necklace back into Melony's hand, "you need to leave while you have that chance."

It was very well known among Desalians that any man or woman who turned their alliance against the kingdom would bear the penalty of death. But it seemed, whether Melony remained here or not, she'd have her life to defend.

"How do I know Hydia will be any better?" Melony asked in her own whisper.

Melinda didn't need to think long for her answer. "How could it be worse?"

That was the question Melony repeated in her mind when she left to help her Desalians against the attack, when she found herself facing the 'Hydian maid' called Alexria, and when she stood on the ship escaping Desali. How could Hydia be any worse? At first she thought the answer to that question was Miken. Adicara had wagered earlier that the prisoners would only be able to escape if the new Guardians of Hydia were among them. Seeing Miken fighting with a mask and the 'Hydian maid' joining him, Melony had connected the pieces herself. Miken hadn't reacted well to being called a Guardian of Hydia and this confused her. If Miken wasn't Desalian and wasn't Hydian than what was he? How was she supposed to act around him?

When they arrived on the shore of Hydia, Melony had expected to travel with Alexria, but having Miken's critical eye on her everyday was difficult to adjust to. She found that the less she said, the less likely she'd say something wrong. So Melony spent her days following and watching and doing what she was told to do. They travelled all across Hydia, helping a village here and a family there. Melony expected the Guardians of Hydia to steadily be hunting down Desalians, but they weren't. In the first several days Melony was with them, Miken and Alexria never drew their blades at all.

It was twelve days after they left Desali that Melony learned why Hydia was a worse life for her. The three of them were passing through a village to buy and barter supplies. Melony waited with the horses while Miken and Alexria dealt with the market men. She propped herself up on the top rung of a fence and let her feet dangle. Her horse watched her.

"Well, at least you're safe to talk to," Melony said to the horse.

Her gaze drifted to a man in the crowd walking toward her. Her stomach tightened when she recognized him. It was Adicara. Miken and Alexria were now several strides away and with their backs to her. Trying to run would be useless. So was calling out for help. She'd be dead in moments if she tried either. Adicara hadn't drawn any weapons yet, so maybe that was a good sign. He did always seem to take interest in her.

"I must say, Melony," Adicara said as he reached her, "you certainly impressed me." He sat on one of the lower fence rungs so the horses blocked him from Miken and Alexria's view.

"I wasn't expecting to see you here," Melony said, trying to match the casual tone he spoke with.

"When Sinele found out you left, he wanted me to kill you," Adicara said. "However, once I explained your plan to spy on the Guardians of Hydia, he was just as impressed as I was."

A spy? Would it kill her to say she wasn't?

"I'm sure I'm not the first to do it," Melony said. It was hard to keep her voice from shaking.

"You're the first Desalian who the Guardians of Hydia trust," Adicara said. His calm, casual voice was steady. "A position like that is too valuable to pass up."

Yes, it would kill her to say she wasn't here to spy.

"Then I'm glad you're on my side," Melony said.

Adicara stood to leave. "You'll see me again. I look forward to hearing what you learn."

"Adicara," Melony said suddenly. There was one question that had been hovering on her mind for the last twelve days. She couldn't bring herself to ask Alexria and especially not Miken. But Adicara always seemed to be knowledgeable in rumours and information. "When I was a child," she asked, "who took me from Alexria? Did Sular do it himself?"

Before turning to walk away, Adicara said, "Trust me, Melony. If I knew I'd tell you."

www.ingramcontent.com/pod-product-compliance
Lightning Source LLC
Chambersburg PA
CBHW070108260626
47160CB00004B/1381